MW01534629

REFUGE OF REDEMPTION

FOG LAKE: THE COLSONS

CHRISTY BARRITT

River Heights

CHAPTER
ONE

THEY DON'T KNOW *what they don't know.*

As I sit among my colleagues, the reminder makes me smile.

A little too widely.

Just as the thought crosses my mind, my phone buzzes with a notification. Even though I'm in a meeting, I pick it up and click the button. I fully expect to see a deer. Maybe even a bear or a park ranger.

Instead, I spot three women with backpacks and heavy winter jackets traipsing through the forest, the trio reminding me a tad of Little Red Riding Hood— only tripled.

They look like they know exactly where they're going.

I knew this day might come. I've been planning for it for a long time. Safeguards are in place.

You see, I have hunting cameras positioned at several places in the woods. An alert is sent to me whenever something or someone walks past. I monitor them all I can.

No one must find my secret place.

At the first sign that someone is too close, I jump into action. Once, some hikers were in the area and I rushed to intercept them and feigned a sprained ankle. The group had to escort me back to my car. Another time, I saw park rangers heading that way, so I called in a fire at another part of the forest. Though it had been a false alarm, they'd abandoned that area and hadn't returned since.

I could always think of some way to outsmart them. It's what I do.

No one will stand in my way.

Especially not now—because now it's my turn.

Now this is all about me.

I remember the last message I had been given: *Activate.*

Finally, I have the opportunity to present a plot twist that no one will forget.

And I plan on making the most of it.

My heart pounds in my ears.

I zoom in on the video on my phone, seeing if I can make out any more details.

"Is everything okay?" my boss asks me from the front of the conference table.

I quickly put my phone back into my pocket and nod, trying to look like the faithful employee I've been all these years. Not a single write-up or strike against me in my records. I need to keep it that way.

I force a smile. "Sorry about that. I got a false alarm on my home security system."

My boss nods and gets back to the presentation at hand.

But I can't get the image out of my mind.

I recognize one of those women.

I've followed her career ever since she crashed and burned for the public to see.

My heart pounds harder.

There's only one reason she'd be in that area right now.

And I know what it is.

She's discovered my secret.

Tension embeds itself in my back as I realize what's at stake.

I need to do something. Now. Before it's too late.

I stand, rather abruptly, and hold my phone up. "Actually, my security system went off again. I need to check everything out at my house . . . if you don't mind."

My boss nods, totally clueless. "Of course. I hope everything is okay. I'll fill you in later on anything you miss."

Perfect.

Because I might be gone for longer than anyone anticipates.

CHAPTER
TWO

"ARE you sure we should be here?"

Piper Stephens barely heard her friend as she dodged another skeletal tree branch while trudging up the steep mountain. The hike was far more challenging than she'd imagined. The optimist in her always liked to believe that things would be easier than they actually were.

"Piper?" Julie repeated.

Julie Anderson, Piper's assistant, had come along with Piper as well as Luna Fisher, Piper's intern. The three of them had driven down this morning from Lexington, Kentucky, to Fog Lake, Tennessee, for the outing.

They'd only stay for an hour or two before heading back. The last thing Piper wanted was to navigate these mountain roads in the dark.

Piper cleared her throat before using another branch to help pull herself up the rugged mountainside. "Look, even if The Good Samaritan Killer *did* have an apprentice—which I'm nearly certain is true —it's not like he's going to station himself in the middle of nowhere just watching and waiting for anyone to come along and discover his secrets."

Piper tried to sound certain. But on the inside, she asked herself the same questions.

Was it a good idea to hike an hour and a half into this secluded area?

There were three of them—so safety in numbers.

But still.

This whole area somehow felt haunted. Not that she believed in ghosts. She didn't.

It was just that . . . when so many crimes had been committed in one town, how could someone not feel eerie being here?

Piper had considered telling the FBI about her possible discovery. But, right now, she was simply acting on a hunch. She needed to figure out if she was really onto something or not before she shared her theory.

Especially after that last incident . . . the one that had gotten her fired and blacklisted from every law enforcement agency within sixty miles. Now, she had to prove herself or lose what was left of her miserable career.

Equal parts fear and excitement shimmied through her blood as she thought about what today might hold.

Fear that she was making a mistake.

Excitement that she might discover evidence offering more answers.

At least she wasn't alone.

Julie was brilliant in so many ways, and, in other ways, she was Piper's complete opposite. Where Piper let her creativity rule, Julie always followed logic. Julie even dressed pragmatically in her jeans, LL Bean sweatshirt, and well-worn hiking boots.

In the middle of planning the trip, Luna had asked if she could also come along. Luna was only nineteen, with light-brown skin and long, dark hair. Since Luna was an avid mountain hiker, Piper figured her extensive experience could only be an asset.

They'd already hiked two miles through the Smoky Mountains in thirty-degree weather. They weren't on a marked trail. Instead, they were using a map and a compass to guide them.

There were all kinds of warning signs that this was a bad idea.

For starters, the past three times Piper had checked, she had no cell phone service.

Despite that, the eternal optimist in her told her that everything would be fine.

They only had a half-mile more to go, then they should be at the site. As soon as they checked the area out, the three of them would head back and should be at Piper's car well before sunset.

What could go wrong?

"You really think we might find something here?" Luna paused several feet in front of them, not looking winded at all.

Piper tried not to breathe too hard and show just how out of shape she was. Though she worked out on an elliptical three times a week—at least, she *tried* to when she didn't get consumed by projects—the workout machine really didn't compare to actual hiking, especially with the air as thin and cold as it was now.

"I'm hopeful," Piper answered, making sure to sound positive.

She'd been studying the crime-scene photos taken in regard to The Good Samaritan Killer as well as examining each of the videos he'd posted of himself "saving" his victims.

Photo analysis was her specialty. Not only did she take crime-scene photos and study them, but she examined other photos to see if they were altered in any way. She was a noted expert in enhancing and enlarging images in order to possibly pick up clues not initially seen by investigators.

In the process of doing that with the GSK photos, Piper had noticed several peculiar things.

Including one of a map with an X marked on it.

It was in the photo that had been taken of Loretta Pascal when she'd died in an "auto accident." She'd been The Good Samaritan Killer's fourth victim.

Investigators probably hadn't thought much about the map because it was contained in a mix of other objects that had fallen from the glove compartment during her accident.

But Piper thought it could be a clue. That's why they were here.

Finally, the three of them crested the ridge they'd been climbing, and a relatively flat landscape stretched before them—for twenty feet or so at least.

As her breath frosted in the air in front of her, Piper pulled out the updated map she'd printed for this trip and glanced at it again. "We should be close. Really close."

"Actually, we're right *here*." Luna pointed at a different area on the map, probably two inches from where Piper pointed.

"Oh." Piper tried to hide her embarrassment.

How could she be so brilliant in some areas of her life and such a ditz in others? "But if that's right . . ."

Julie nodded at a rock formation rising in the distance, her auburn hair—pulled into a practical ponytail—bobbing with the action. "Then that's where we're headed."

Piper's heart pounded harder.

She took several more steps and paused.

Beneath her hiking boots were some old train tracks that probably hadn't been used in three decades. Not since the mines in this area had shut down.

This was it.

This was the moment Piper would find out if her theory was correct.

Even though it was still daylight, everything felt darker up here. Perhaps it was because of the skeletal trees around her or the shadow of the mountains in the distance.

A nervous energy filled the air as they began following the rails.

As they rounded the bend, Piper sucked in a breath.

A large opening in the mountainside gaped at her.

An old mine.

Not many people knew the tunnel was up here, and it wasn't exactly easy to get to anymore.

But they'd found it.

They'd found it!

"You guys . . ." Piper muttered. "There it is."

"Should we really do this?" Julie stared at the black hole, her skin looking a little paler.

"We'll just go inside and take a peek," Piper said. "We won't go so far that we can't see the light at the opening. At the first sign of trouble—which I'm not anticipating—we'll leave. But if either of you guys don't want to do this with me, then I understand—"

"I'm in." Luna's eyes lit up. "I can't wait to see what's in there."

Julie blew out a breath. "I'm in also, but I'm chickening out if I hear any movement inside. Bats. Vagabonds. Killers."

"That sounds fair enough." Piper gripped her flashlight tighter.

As she got closer to the opening, cool air billowed out from the depths of the mountain, and she shivered.

Piper told herself it was because of the cold. But she was nervous too, whether she admitted it aloud or not.

She quickened her steps and took the lead, studying the metal fence strung across the opening and the "No Trespassing" signs.

Piper wouldn't trespass without a good reason.

But her motive—the theory she was testing out—had the power to change people's lives. In this case, disobeying the law was worth the risk.

Drawing in a deep breath, Piper slipped through an opening in the gate, careful not to snag her jacket on the rusty links.

She took the first step inside the old tunnel, ignoring the internal voice that urged her to turn around.

Darkness surrounded her on all sides. Some old wooden boxes were strewn on the edges of the space, the dirt covering them making them appear as if they hadn't been touched in years. Wood beams held up the walls and ceiling, and a small, dead critter lay in a state of decomposition only a couple of feet away.

She took a few steps farther.

"Look at that." Luna pointed at something with her flashlight.

Piper swung her gaze in that direction, and her eyes widened.

An old purse slumped against the rock wall.

It looked old, but not *that* old.

Besides, the miners who used to work up here? Piper doubted any of them carried beaded pink purses.

A touch of trepidation filled Piper.

Despite that, she snapped a picture of it with her professional-grade camera.

"What do you think?" Julie glanced at Piper, her eyes as wide as saucers. Clearly, worst-case scenarios were going through her head.

"I'm just going to walk a little farther," Piper said. "From what I read about this place, this shaft branches off into several different tunnels that wind deep into the mountain."

"Is there only one way in and one way out?" Julie asked.

"No, but this is the main entrance." Piper had researched the place as much as she could before coming. "From what I read, the mine has several vents also that keep air moving through the space."

"I hate the dark." Julie visibly shivered again.

Piper's nose and fingertips felt like ice cubes as she continued forward. With every new step, darkness seemed to cocoon her even more.

She shivered, the action nearly making her teeth chatter. But she tried to use a Jedi mind trick on herself to hide her chill.

If she showed just the slightest touch of fear, Julie and Luna just might abandon this whole expedition.

They paused where the tunnel split into two narrow corridors. More evidence of past mining operations littered the area around them. Old shovels, hand drills, hard hats.

"I don't think we should go any farther." Julie stopped and grabbed Piper's arm. "There's no telling what's down there. I can barely see the light at the opening from here."

Julie glanced behind her at the fading daylight.

Piper understood where Julie was coming from. But Piper hadn't come all the way up here to turn back so soon. She had no idea if or when she might make it here again.

Aside from the purse, there was no evidence here of anything except mining.

But that didn't fit the scenarios in her mind. If Piper's theory was correct, very bad things had happened in this space.

"I'm just going to take a couple of steps down into this tunnel," Piper murmured.

"Piper . . ." Julie warned.

"You stay there," Luna insisted. "Like Piper said, we'll just take a little peek to see if there's anything of note."

Piper tried to quell the nerves inside her as she stepped forward.

But the darkness felt so overwhelming.

She paused after several steps and let her light fill the area.

Piper's beam stopped on something in the distance. "What is that?"

"You see something?" Luna stepped closer.

"I think so."

Side by side, they slowly approached the object.

As Piper got closer, she knelt beside the mystery item and took a few pictures to preserve what the scene looked like.

Then she took a small shovel from her backpack and gently began to scrape away the dirt around it.

Her mind reeled at what she saw.

"It's a skull . . ." Piper muttered.

Luna gasped and staggered backward until she collided with the wall. "No . . ."

Piper's heart pounded harder.

She'd thought she wanted to prove her theory. But now that she was here and seeing the truth, she wondered if coming here had ever been a good idea at all.

"Julie, you won't believe this." Piper shone her light back toward the entrance of the tunnel, expecting to see her friend there.

But she saw nothing.

Had Julie been so frightened that she'd run from the tunnel?

It didn't seem like something her friend would do. But maybe.

"What should we do now?" Luna turned toward Piper with wide eyes.

Piper rose, her gaze going back to the skull. "I need to let the FBI know. But first . . ."

She took several more pictures. She couldn't be certain, but she felt sure other bones jutted out of the dirt. That those weren't rocks.

The realization made her head spin.

"Come on," Piper said. "We can't stay much longer anyway. I don't want to be out here when it starts getting dark."

They hurried out of the smaller tunnel. But when they reached the main corridor where they left Julie, she was gone.

Piper shone her light around again. "Julie?"

Still nothing.

Even if Julie had run, could she not hear them now? Or had she started running and been unable to stop?

Piper and Luna exchanged a glance, but neither of them voiced any theories out loud. Not yet.

Instead, they hurried toward the daylight beckoning them in the distance.

When they slipped between the links of the fence, Julie wasn't there either.

"Julie!" Piper shouted, listening as her voice echoed over the mountains.

Worry began to creep up her spine.

"Piper . . ." Luna glanced around, not bothering to hide the fear in her gaze.

Piper looked back at the tunnel. "I'm going to have to go back in there. Maybe Julie went down the other tunnel."

"That doesn't seem like something that she would do, not given her fear of the dark."

"I agree. But I don't know what else to do. We can't leave without her." Piper's heart pounded harder, and her lungs tightened until she could hardly breathe.

How had things spiraled out of control so quickly?

They'd hiked to the location without incident and found the evidence that she expected.

But now Julie . . .

"Julie!" Piper shouted again.

She prayed her friend would respond. That this was all some type of misunderstanding.

But as Piper glanced around, she still didn't see Julie.

"I've got to go back inside and look for her," she muttered.

Luna grabbed her arm and squeezed hard. "You're not leaving me out here. But I don't want to go in very far."

"We won't. All we need is for all of us to disappear or get lost." Even as she said the words, they somehow served as a reminder of how deadly this situation could turn.

She wanted to believe that Julie would appear from around the corner and tell them she'd just slipped behind a tree to go to the bathroom or something.

But, deep in her gut, Piper knew that wasn't the case.

This made no sense.

Julie wasn't the type to go off on her own.

Piper paused at the split in the tunnel and stared down the opposite one, the one she hadn't yet explored.

As she shone her light on the ground, her beam swept across something that hadn't been there before.

Julie's cell phone.

The screen had been smashed, almost as if she'd dropped it.

Or as if someone had destroyed it on purpose.

CHAPTER
THREE

BEAR COLSON HAD JUST FINISHED TEACHING his online cyber criminology class when his phone buzzed.

He glanced at the screen, and his heart skipped a beat when he saw Piper Stephens' name. He'd been hoping to hear from her again. He looked forward to it a little more than he should.

He grabbed the phone to answer, reminding himself to stay casual before he hit Talk. "Hey, Piper."

"Bear! Is . . . that you?"

The voice sounded like Piper's, but the connection was terrible, with static and crackling. He could barely make out what she was saying.

"Piper? Are you okay?" He sat up straighter in his desk chair and waited for her response.

"I . . . you."

He stood and paced toward his office door, desperate for a better connection. "What's going on?"

"Mine . . . gone."

What in the world was Piper talking about? Had she lost something?

"911."

Bear's heart pounded harder.

No, she hadn't lost something. Piper needed help.

His back went rigid. "Where are you, Piper?"

"Elk . . . mine."

What was she talking about?

"The . . . North Elk Ridge . . . Mine."

Then it hit him.

One of the old mines in the area was the North Elk Ridge. The abandoned site was only about a fifteen-minute drive from his house—and the rest of the way he'd have to hike.

What was Piper doing there? He didn't know, but now didn't seem like the time to ask. Not when she sounded so desperate.

"I'll be there as quickly as I can." Bear grabbed his boots from the closet and began tugging them on.

He didn't get a response.

"Piper? Are you there?" He paused for just a moment.

But there was still nothing.

They must have lost their connection.

He quickly tied his boots. As he headed down-stairs, he called Fog Lake Sheriff Luke Wilder. Wilder told him that Piper had already been able to get a call in to 911, and they were getting a rescue crew orga-nized. But it would take them a while to get the off-road vehicles ready and closer to the site.

Bear would be able to get there more quickly than the sheriff.

He dashed out the door, hopped in his truck, and headed down the road.

When Bear had woken this morning, more snow had covered the ground. It had been snowier than usual this winter. Usually, he loved it. But not when he was in a hurry.

Slippery, icy roads and urgency didn't mesh.

He tried to temper himself as he headed down the narrow mountain road.

He hadn't heard about North Elk Ridge Mine in a long time. Thirty years ago, the place had been one of the primary sources of employment in the area. But several accidents had shut it down.

Now, mostly only old-timers knew it was there. The roads leading to it had become overgrown, making the place inaccessible except on foot or ORV.

But Bear's father had taken him there once when he was a kid. They'd gone on a weekend hiking trip, and his father had shown him the old mine entrance before warning him about the dangers of ever going inside a place like that.

A chill washed over him at the memory.

This place . . . it wasn't tied in some way with The Good Samaritan Killer, was it?

Bear shook his head. No . . . that would be too much of a coincidence.

He continued down the road until he spotted a silver sedan parked on the side. The out-of-state Kentucky plates confirmed to him who the vehicle must belong to.

Piper Stephens.

One of the most intriguing women he had ever met.

What in the world was she doing out here? Why hadn't she told Bear she'd be in the area?

A pang of disappointment rushed through him, but he shoved it aside.

His own feelings weren't important right now.

Instead, he parked and grabbed the backpack from behind his seat. He always kept it with him just in case, stocked with emergency supplies. It had come in handy on more than one occasion.

Pulling the straps over his shoulders, he started toward a path leading up the side of the mountain. He knew the marked hike, which was part of a different trail, wouldn't last long and that soon he'd be on his own.

Thankfully, he kept himself in shape. Circuit training, weights, and daily cardio was essential for him, especially since he worked a desk job at home. He'd set up his own exercise room in his climate-controlled garage and liked to head out there first thing in the morning.

He moved quickly through the trees, climbing rocks, and avoiding icy patches as he ascended.

Bear had always had a good sense of direction, and he'd glanced at his map before he left. He felt confident he was heading the right way.

It took him forty minutes to hike two and a half miles up the mountain and reach the site of the old mine.

Forty minutes that felt more like forty hours.

But, finally, he was here.

He hurried down the old railroad tracks toward the mine entrance.

As he did, he spotted two women near the gated opening of the mine.

One of them was Piper.

He'd recognize her slim figure, chin-length straight brown hair, and pert features anywhere.

As Piper looked up and spotted him, she hurried his way and threw her arms around him.

Bear only hesitated a moment before returning her embrace.

He'd often dreamed what this might be like.

But he'd never expected it to happen like this.

Still, he reminded himself not to let down his guard. Everyone he'd ever trusted in his life had let him down. And given Piper's past . . . trusting her was risky.

Too risky.

Still, he held her close a moment, every protective instinct in him flaring to life.

When she finally pulled away, he asked, "What happened?"

As he waited for her to answer, Bear soaked in her red-rimmed eyes. She was shaken and scared. Probably cold too. The temperature had dropped into the mid-twenties.

"My friend . . . Julie." She rubbed her throat as she swallowed hard, clearly trying to gather herself.

He glanced over at the woman with Piper, wondering if she was who Piper was talking about.

Piper seemed to read his mind and swung her head back and forth.

"That's Luna, my intern. Julie is my assistant. She disappeared. Into thin air. I can't find her anywhere. I don't know what to do." Piper's words came out fast and high-pitched.

Bear's spine stiffened, and he wanted to pull Piper into another hug. But he needed to figure out what had happened first.

"Law enforcement will be here soon. In the meantime, I'll see if I can find your friend. She went in there, right?"

He stepped toward the mine entrance.

Before he could go any farther, Piper clutched his arm. "You can't go in there. It's too dangerous."

"I'll be okay." Bear liked spelunking and doing other adventurous, outdoorsy activities on the weekends. This wasn't his first rodeo.

Moisture glistened in Piper's eyes as she stared up at him. "You don't understand. I think The Good Samaritan Killer's apprentice may have taken her."

Her words echoed in his head a moment.

The Good Samaritan Killer?

Bear had prayed that nightmare was behind him. He prayed his theories were wrong. That this was really over. That the Understudy didn't really exist.

But what if it wasn't?

What if the GSK was like a stain on his life . . . a stain that would never go away?

CHAPTER
FOUR

PIPER HAD JUST CONVINCED Bear not to go into the mine when she heard the roar of engines in the distance.

ORVs, if she had to guess. That was probably how law enforcement traveled to secluded areas.

She'd called them before she called Bear. She had to climb overtop the mine in order to find even one bar of service—but she was thankful for that one bar.

Why had she called Bear after she talked to 911?

She wasn't sure. She only knew she'd found comfort in his presence before. Plus, this was his home turf, and she could use someone local on her side right now. As she stood next to him, she knew she'd made the right choice.

Bear kept a hand on her elbow, almost as if he feared she might pass out.

The man had been so unexpected when she'd met him the first time. She'd anticipated someone . . . well, someone nerdy and bookish. Not that it mattered to her what the man looked like. Their relationship was purely professional.

But he had lived up to his name. Bear Colson was probably six foot four with broad, muscular shoulders, and a chest that stretched on for miles. His eyes were striking green and intensely intelligent. His dark hair was long enough to be tied back at the nape of his neck. At one time, he'd had a full beard. Now only a day's growth appeared on his cheeks and upper lip.

Not only that, but his voice was deep, his actions sure, and he could intimidate anyone he came across with just one look.

Not exactly your average, everyday professor.

A moment later, law enforcement pulled onto the scene. Six men came altogether, a mix of law enforcement from the sheriff's department, the park service, and state police.

A man in a sheriff's uniform climbed from an ORV and strode toward them. He appeared to be in his early thirties with dark brown hair and a serious demeanor.

The rest of the crew headed toward the mine as if ready to begin searching.

The sheriff exchanged a few words with Bear before turning toward her.

"I'm Fog Lake Sheriff Luke Wilder," he started. "You're Piper?"

She nodded, panic trying to claim her as the reality of the situation hit her again. Her gaze skittered across the open expanse to Luna, who stood off by herself.

Piper knew she couldn't take her eyes off her. What if she did and Luna disappeared also?

She swallowed hard and turned back toward the sheriff. "Piper Stephens. I'm a crime-scene photographer and photo analyst."

"You work for a department?"

"I'm currently a contractor, sir."

"You do realize you weren't supposed to be in that mine, don't you?" The sheriff stared at her as he waited for her response.

"I do. But it was important that I go inside." Impatience rose in her. She knew the best law enforcement officers remained calm in situations like these. But she felt like he should be in that tunnel looking for her friend right now instead of questioning her.

He narrowed his eyes as if skeptical. "What was so important?"

Piper nibbled on her bottom lip as she thought

about her response. This wasn't the way she wanted to report her discovery. This wasn't the way she'd pictured explaining the hours she'd put into this case.

But Julie's life was on the line right now, so it wasn't a time to wax poetic about her work.

"I . . ." She swallowed hard. "I found some evidence that indicated The Good Samaritan Killer may have left something of importance inside that mine."

The sheriff cocked an eyebrow as he studied her. "The Good Samaritan Killer is behind bars. He was arrested two weeks ago. Ralph Burgess. He pulled the wool over all our eyes."

Piper nibbled her lip again. "I know, but . . . I think he had someone helping him. An apprentice, I suppose."

Sheriff Wilder's jaw tightened, and he glanced at the old mine entrance. "Is your friend the type who would just take off?"

Level-headed Julie filled her thoughts. "No, not at all. She hates the dark."

"Then what do you think happened?"

"I think someone took her." She raised her chin, knowing exactly how she sounded. But she didn't care. She wasn't crazy.

The sheriff's eyebrows climbed higher. "Who?"

"I don't know."

He glanced at the tunnel. "My team is in there now, getting a preliminary look at the scene. Do you have a picture of your friend?"

She pulled one up on her phone and showed him.

"I'll need a copy of that," Sheriff Wilder said and gave her his direct contact number.

"I'll send it now. One more thing." Piper squirmed before sharing the next piece of information. "When you go in, you have to be careful. There are . . . dead bodies."

————

As Bear stood near the tunnel entrance, he could hardly believe what Piper had said.

Couldn't believe Piper was here.

Couldn't believe . . . any of this.

"Dead bodies?" He turned toward Piper, a sudden desperate need hitting him—a need to find more details.

Piper swallowed and rubbed her throat as she glanced into the abyss beside them. "I found a skull, but I believe there are more bones and human remains."

Sheriff Wilder plucked his radio from his belt. "I'm going to need to call the FBI in for this."

Bear's mind reeled. He'd suspected for a while that The Good Samaritan Killer had an apprentice—or an understudy, as he liked to call him.

The man was given the name because he recorded himself supposedly saving victims from various tragic situations like car accidents or near drownings. But in reality, he caused those very incidents. And after he recorded himself saving the women?

He killed them and branded them with GSK under the tender flesh of their arm. He left a silver cross behind to make it clear he was responsible. Then he posted his rescue videos online, each time using a different IP address. Eventually people found them, and praise flowed in.

Only he didn't deserve any praise.

The man was a cold-blooded killer. So far, seven murders had been attributed to the monster.

Bear's dad had been accused of the crimes and sent to prison. But he'd been set up. Just recently, the real killer had been apprehended.

Then, a couple of weeks ago, Bear and Piper had studied the man's videos. He'd ask her to look into them and use her equipment to clarify some images.

In doing so, they'd discovered a subtle difference in the videos the man posted. In two of the videos, the man's left hand didn't match. One had a small scar near the thumb.

Bear's heart pounded harder.

Was this the proof they needed that the Understudy really did exist?

If so, he never wanted *this* to happen in order to get that confirmation.

"You stay here." Sheriff Wilder gave Piper and Bear a stern look. "I'm going to get an update from the rest of the team."

"Yes, sir," Piper muttered.

As they waited, Bear glanced at Luna as she stood near the edge of the woods. She looked paler now than she had only moments before. Bear wished he had something to offer other than water and granola bars. But he also knew it would take more than food and water to fix this situation.

Only time would help the shock wear off.

He glanced at the sky. They only had a couple of hours until sunset, and the trek from this place would be dangerous after dark. They all needed to keep that in mind.

Luna continued pacing, going back and forth from the tunnel entrance to Piper. When she was out of earshot, Bear leaned closer to Piper and murmured, "Why didn't you tell me you were coming up here?"

She looked up at him, her gaze luminous yet tortured. "I didn't want to be the girl who cried wolf. I wanted to make sure."

"How did you even know to look here?" Bear glanced back at the tunnel, his mind still racing.

Piper sighed before running a hand through her hair. "It's . . . well, it's a long story. But I'll tell you about it. I'll show you. But when we're away from here, okay?"

"Of course."

Several minutes later, Sheriff Wilder strode back toward them. "We've searched the first half a mile or so inside. We were assured those areas were safe. We found the bones you were talking about. The FBI is coming to see what can be recovered."

"And Julie?" Piper's voice cracked with hopefulness.

A grim line pulled at Sheriff Wilder's lips. "Nothing yet. But we did find some footprints in the east tunnel."

"One set or two?"

A frown flickered across the sheriff's face before he said, "Two."

A cry seemed to gurgle in Piper's throat, and Bear slipped his arm around her shoulder again, afraid she might collapse.

"Oh, Julie . . . this is my fault." She pinched the skin between her eyes.

"You couldn't have known." Bear tried to assure her.

"It just doesn't make any sense. No one knew we were coming. Was someone just hiding out here, waiting for us to show up?"

"We're going to figure that out," Sheriff Wilder said. "I'm sure the FBI will want to question you, but that can wait until after we search the scene. Where are you from?"

"Lexington, Kentucky."

"You'll need to stay in town for the night. The best thing you can do right now is to head back before it gets dark. You and Miss Fisher both need to warm up and get some rest."

"But—" Piper started.

"I know you want to stay." Sheriff Wilder's voice turned sterner. "But there's nothing else you can do here. We'll call you with updates and questions."

Her shoulders remained tense, but finally she nodded. "Okay."

"I can walk them down," Bear said. "My truck is parked on the side of the road."

"Thanks, Bear. I'd appreciate that."

Without wasting any more time, Bear nodded toward the woods in the distance. "We should get started. We don't have any time to waste, and you don't want to be out after dark. It's not safe."

Piper sucked in a breath at his words.

Maybe he should have worded it differently.

Then again, he'd only been telling the truth.

CHAPTER
FIVE

PIPER AND LUNA were quiet as they headed down the road in Bear's steel-gray Toyota Tundra. They'd decided to leave Piper's car parked on the side of the mountain road and come back later to get it. She wasn't in the right frame of mind to drive right now—not if she wanted to arrive in one piece.

Piper stared out the window as twilight began to fall in the Smoky Mountains. She'd always loved these mountains. But, right now, they almost seemed creepy.

How could this have happened? Nothing made sense.

Julie . . . sweet Julie.

What if she was in pain right now? Or scared?

She had to be *so* scared.

This wasn't what her assistant had signed up for.

Julie had come to Piper to learn the basics of crime-scene photography and investigation.

And now this . . .

"Don't beat yourself up." Bear's voice cut through her solemn thoughts.

"How can I not?" Piper continued to stare out the window, afraid if she looked at him that she might completely break down.

"You couldn't have known," Luna said quietly from the backseat. "No one is blaming you except you."

"I should have just told the police what I thought I'd discovered, what I was thinking. But this was just a theory and—"

"No one could have anticipated what happened today," Bear said.

Piper pinched the skin between her eyes as more thoughts collided in her mind. "I need to call Julie's parents. Or do the police do that? I should be the one to tell them—"

Bear gently raised a hand, signaling for her to calm down. "Just slow your thoughts a moment. You can ask the FBI when they talk to you. You don't want to jump the gun on this."

She crossed her arms over her chest, still fighting anxiety.

Bear was right. Piper couldn't panic right now.

Panicking wouldn't help anyone find her friend. She took a few deep breaths and let them out slowly, trying to calm her nerves.

Several minutes later, they pulled to a stop in front of a lonely but impressive house in the middle of a fortress of mountains. The two-story structure with its stone siding and deep-blue shutters looked inviting—like the kind of place that should have children playing outside and a puppy frolicking after them.

"Where are we?" Piper asked.

Bear stared in front of him and shrugged. "This is my place. I thought it might feel homier than a hotel. I probably should have asked first, but you seemed to have a lot on your mind."

Bear's place. The man continued to surprise her—in good ways. *Very* good ways. "No, this is great. At least, until I can figure out what's next. Is this okay with you, Luna?"

"Anywhere is fine," she said. "I'm just ready to get warm."

"Perfect." He put his truck in Park. "Let's get you both inside and out of the cold. I have some soup in the crockpot."

Soup in the crockpot? This guy looked like Jason Momoa, cooked like Martha Stewart, and was as smart as a cyber-savvy Sherlock Holmes.

Piper needed to be careful and keep her distance. Because Bear Colson seemed exactly like the man of her dreams.

The last time she'd fallen for someone, her heart had been broken and her career ruined.

She couldn't let that happen again . . . no matter how tempting Bear Colson might be.

———

Up until a few months ago, Bear hardly ever had anyone over to his place. But recently, his house had practically become a bed-and-breakfast.

First, his sister, Madison, had stayed with him. Then his brother, Isaac. Then Isaac's girlfriend, Rebecca.

It appeared Bear was destined to learn the fine art of hospitality. Although, he wasn't a hermit like people thought, he did prefer to keep his private life private. But he still found time to participate with his hiking club, to go skiing with some friends every December in Colorado, and to catch at least one NFL game in person every year.

Inside, as they hung their coats on hooks behind the door, the scent of potato soup hit him. He would start a fire also—right after he showed the women to his spare bedrooms. They could either change, unwind, or sleep overnight if that's what they wanted.

He'd feel better knowing they were somewhere safe instead of at a hotel by themselves—especially considering what had happened. But it was their decision.

"I need to call my mom . . ." Luna muttered as she stood at the base of the stairs. A nervous ripple shook her voice. "I need to tell her what happened."

If Bear had to guess, the woman was in college. She didn't exactly look terrified. But she seemed stoic, and behind that stoic expression was probably a lot of trepidation. Anyone would feel that way in her shoes.

"Do what you need to do." He showed them up to the bedrooms and then came back to the kitchen to check on his soup.

But his thoughts raced as he worked.

Any day now, his father was supposed to be released from prison. Apparently, it was a longer process than anyone had anticipated.

The real Good Samaritan Killer was now behind bars and awaiting trial. That meant his dad should be free.

Bear was thrilled his dad would finally be exonerated and that justice would be served. But that wouldn't automatically fix the tension between the two of them, especially since they'd recently learned about new evidence that could have cleared his father years earlier. His dad hadn't been forthright about a woman he'd been secretly seeing. Instead, James Colson had chosen to go to prison while his children had been left in the care of an abusive aunt.

That realization still stung.

Even once his dad came home, it wasn't like the Colsons would be one big, happy family again. They would take family therapy to a whole new level.

Now this . . .

When would this nightmare end?

Where was Piper's friend, Julie?

A bad feeling brewed in Bear's gut.

He couldn't wait to talk to Piper more. To hear what had led her to that old mine. To pick her brain about what was going on.

Because there was far more to this situation than what met the eye.

Somehow, his life was interminably entangled in this mess—though it had never been by his choice.

CHAPTER
SIX

AN HOUR LATER, Luna and Piper had showered and changed into some spare clothes Bear's sister kept at the house. They'd been fed. Now, Luna's parents were on their way to pick her up.

Meanwhile, Special Agent Shane Townsend from the FBI had arrived. Bear had gotten to know him fairly well over the past several months, and he knew Shane was one of the good guys.

Piper and Luna sat in chairs near the fireplace. Piper had tight lines across her forehead as she related to Agent Townsend what had happened. Bear stood behind her, close enough to be a support if necessary—and to hear the details about her discovery.

Piper licked her lips before continuing. "Julie . . .

she's great. Quiet. Studious. Curious. She asked if she could work for me, so I said yes."

"Work for you doing what?" Shane leaned toward Piper, his gaze intense as he listened closely to everything she said.

"I'm a forensic photographer and image specialist," Piper explained. "I'm an independent contractor right now, but I worked for the Chicago PD for five years."

Shane narrowed his eyes as if trying to conjure up a memory. "Your name sounds familiar."

"I helped solve the AJ Winders case." Piper nibbled on her bottom lip.

Bear knew all about that case. Most people did.

The police hadn't been able to figure out who had killed a string of suburban housewives. But Piper had a knack for taking pictures of things that no one else thought to look at, including the crowds that were drawn to crime scenes.

While doing so, Piper noticed that the same man appeared at different crimes, disguised differently in each one. The police had identified the man as AJ Winders, and Piper's photos had helped the prosecution win their case.

But it was more than that case that had made her name well-known.

Only six months ago, she'd testified that a photo

was authentic. The image was of Daniel Barr and the man he'd killed—Luke Ableton. Barr had claimed he'd never met Ableton before. But the photo changed everything. Because of it, Barr was convicted and sent to prison.

After the sentencing, someone claimed the photo was altered and that Piper had only testified that it was untouched in order to get notoriety for herself.

After more inspection, the photo had been proven to be a fraud.

As a result, the case was thrown out, the convicted killer exonerated, and Piper had been fired.

Piper had proven herself to be a real go-getter. Would she do whatever necessary to get what she wanted? Including compromising her integrity?

Bear reminded himself to keep his distance from her. He'd been betrayed by too many people already.

"How long have you and Julie worked together?" Shane continued.

Piper blew out a breath, her pert features strained under the scrutiny of this conversation. "Just under three months."

"And how did you meet?"

Piper pushed a hair behind her ear, clearly uncomfortable with the questions and the situation. "Julie followed my career online, emailed me, and we got to know each other that way."

Shane nodded and continued to jot down some notes. "What else can you tell me about her?"

"She's twenty-six. She has a degree in business, but she hates it and wants to do something else." Piper shrugged. "I don't know what else I can tell you that might be relevant."

Shane straightened and lowered his notepad. "I think I have enough on Julie for now. Tell me—how did you manage to find these bones in the tunnels?"

Piper drew in a deep breath and glanced at Bear.

He couldn't read the look in her eyes. Hesitation? Apology? Excitement?

"After talking to Bear, I decided to look into the GSK crime-scene photos," Piper started. "I requested copies, and since they're public record anyway . . . I studied those pictures, as well as the videos the GSK posted online. And . . . I think that all along this sicko may have been leaving clues in those photos and in his videos on purpose. It's just that no one put the pieces together."

Bear straightened, his curiosity over where Piper was going with this growing by the second. "And?"

"So, one of the victims, Loretta Pascal, was in a staged car accident. When her body was found, contents of her glove compartment and purse were spilled everywhere. One of the items was an old map with an X marked on it. I'm not sure why no one ever thought to look into it. The X indicated the location of the North Elk Ridge Mine."

"And there's more?" Shane stared at her as he waited for her answer.

Piper rubbed her hands against her jeans and shifted. "I'm . . . I'm not sure. That was my best lead, although I'm examining the photos still. It was through looking at the videos that Bear and I discovered the scar on the man's left hand—*one* of the men's left hands."

"She's been working on this case for weeks," Luna added quietly. "On her own time."

Shane nodded, what appeared to be a touch of admiration in his gaze. "If you discover anything new, I'd appreciate you letting me know."

"Of course."

Before he could say anything else, a knock sounded at the door.

It appeared Luna's parents were here.

But Bear hoped he and Piper could get back to this conversation. He desperately wanted to know what Piper was thinking . . . because he saw something unspoken deep in her gaze.

He knew she was dedicated.

But that didn't mean she wasn't hiding something.

"How could you drag my daughter into a situation like this?" Luna's mom stared at Piper, fire exploding in her eyes.

The woman had just walked into Bear's house, and Piper had gone to the door to greet her. That was as far as it had gone. As soon as Mrs. Fisher had seen Piper, she laid into her.

"Mom, it wasn't like that—" Desperation clung to Luna's words as she reached for her mother.

"Don't interrupt!" Mrs. Fisher's nostrils flared, and her hands went to her slim hips. "Piper is the adult here. She should have known better."

"But I insisted—" Luna started.

"Luna!" Her mother—who looked more like Luna's older sister—stared at her daughter before pointing to the door. "Go outside and wait in the car. I'll be there in a minute."

Piper felt her cheeks heat at the scolding. But she also knew she deserved it. This was her fault. Julie had only been in that mine because of her.

"I'm so sorry, Mrs. Fisher," Piper started after Luna disappeared outside. "I never meant for any of this to happen."

"Luna could be the one missing right now." Mrs. Fisher stared at Piper with an incredulous look in her eyes, as if Piper were a monster with no regard to the safety of others. "All so you could test some theory concerning a killer who's already in jail? I hope you're happy."

Bear stepped forward, only an inch in front of Piper, but his chest seemed to almost be a protective shield. "Piper had no reason to think anyone would be in danger. Otherwise, she wouldn't have gone up to that mine."

Mrs. Fisher's eyes still blazed. "Are you sure about that? Isn't that what got her fired from her other job? The fact that she loves attention and she'll do anything to get it?"

"In all fairness—" Piper started.

Mrs. Fisher turned back toward her, tension tightening her face and shoulders. "I told Luna she shouldn't have anything to do with you, that you were trouble! But she didn't listen to me. I'll make sure she doesn't work for you again. In fact, I'll make sure no one ever works for you again! You've proven yourself to be irresponsible so many times that it's irrefutable!"

Before Piper could respond, Mrs. Fisher stormed outside, slamming the door behind her.

Piper's heart raced as she watched the car pull away, Luna offering a feeble wave from the back seat. Mrs. Fisher's words still echoed in her head. *I told*

Luna she shouldn't have anything to do with you, that you were trouble!

Piper rubbed her throat, feeling a burning sensation. Was that because she feared Mrs. Fisher's words were true? Or because she had been humiliated . . . again? Both Bear and Agent Townsend had been present to witness the accusations tossed at her.

Maybe she was a joke. Maybe she was only pretending to be good at what she did.

Bear squeezed her shoulder. "It's going to be okay."

Piper shook her head. "She's right. The buck stops with me. I was in charge, and I led Julie and Luna into a dangerous situation. I should have known better and taken more precautions—"

"Bear is right." Agent Townsend stepped closer and lowered his voice. "You couldn't have known, Piper. It appears you were in the wrong place at the wrong time."

Piper nodded, but she still didn't feel convinced. No one could make her feel better right now. In fact, she *wouldn't* feel better until Julie was found.

Townsend nodded toward the door, politely quiet as if he wanted to slip out and let Piper deal with the verbal lashing she'd received. "I need to get going."

Bear cleared his throat, his demeanor shifting.

"There's one more thing I want to mention before you go."

"What's that?" Townsend turned toward him, serious lines etched into his face, evident despite his five o'clock shadow.

"As I was hiking back to my truck with Piper and Luna . . . I noticed four different trail cams. I thought it was an odd place for the cams, especially since it's so steep right there—not your ideal hunting location."

"Trail cams?" Townsend nodded slowly as he seemed to process that development. "You're right. That is a strange place to leave those. I'll look into them, see if I can find out who they're registered to. If nothing else, maybe they picked up something."

Piper's heart pounded into her ears.

Trail cams?

Was that how this guy had known they were coming? Had those cameras triggered something and sent a real-time photo or video to someone desperate to keep an eye on the area around the tunnel?

But still, how could anyone get to that mine so quickly? If someone had ridden an ORV, Piper would have heard it.

Things still didn't make sense.

Then she remembered what Townsend had said.

Two sets of footprints led into the east tunnel.

Those prints indicated that Julie hadn't been alone when she disappeared. The footsteps eventually became only one heavier set—probably as someone had carried Julie the rest of the way.

Townsend's phone buzzed, and he glanced at his screen before grunting.

"What is it?" Bear asked.

"They tested Julie's phone screen," Townsend said. "There was evidence of bleach and acetone . . ."

"Chloroform . . . just like what the GSK used . . ." Piper rubbed her forehead. The monster had made a spray out of it, which caused his victims to pass out almost instantaneously.

That explained why Piper hadn't heard anything in the tunnel.

That guy had sneaked up on Julie, sprayed a chemical in her face to make her pass out, and then taken her unconscious body somewhere.

The ice in Piper's core grew colder and colder by the second.

Something was seriously wrong here . . . and her friend was paying the price.

CHAPTER
SEVEN

SPECIAL AGENT TOWNSEND had hardly been gone five minutes when Bear's brother and sister arrived.

Isaac was Bear's younger brother and a Memphis lawyer. Well, not Memphis anymore. He was in the process of moving to Fog Lake and getting back to his roots.

Madison, his younger sister, had started her own nonprofit, Blood and Water, an organization that helped the friends and families of convicted criminals get back on their feet. She had also relocated back to this area recently. She and Special Agent Townsend had practically been inseparable since they met while investigating a copycat killer back in October.

The past several months seemed like such a blur

in so many ways. So much bad had happened . . . yet surprising blessings had popped up in the middle of the ugliness as well.

Bear opened the door and let Isaac and Madison inside then quickly closed it as the brisk wind tried to invade his warm house.

"We heard what happened." Madison tugged her coat off as she looked up at Bear. "We came right away."

"Someone else has been taken?" Isaac rushed.

Before Bear could answer, his siblings glanced behind him and seemed to simultaneously spot Piper. Instantly, their shoulders squared, and their eyes gleamed with curiosity.

"Who's this?" Isaac placed his coat on a hook and turned toward Piper.

Before Bear could introduce her, Piper strode across the room with her arm outstretched. "I'm Piper Stephens."

"I'm Isaac."

"I'm Bear's sister, Madison. It's nice to meet you."

Bear cleared his throat before his brother and sister could jump to conclusions. "Piper is a forensic specialist, and the two of us have been corresponding online for a while. Piper is the one who helped me determine that there were two different men's hands in those videos I showed you."

That fact had led Bear to conclude the Understudy existed.

He and Piper had shared the information with the FBI, but nothing had come of the lead. It seemed like everyone assumed that since this guy hadn't struck in such a long time, that he was in hiding.

But, after today, it didn't seem like that was the case.

"You mind if we grab some soup?" Isaac nodded toward the kitchen. "I could smell it as soon as I walked in, and I'm famished."

"Help yourself," Bear told them.

As Isaac and Madison ladled some soup, Bear fixed drinks for all of them, and a few minutes later they were all seated at the kitchen table.

"So, do you know anything else about what happened today?" Madison asked as she dipped her spoon into the creamy soup. "I wasn't able to talk to Shane very long."

"It's my friend who's missing." Piper's voice cracked.

Piper had been quiet. Probably thinking. Definitely observing. But the light and fire had disappeared from her gaze. She was clearly still shaken— as anyone in her shoes would be.

Madison's eyes instantly softened. "I'm so sorry to hear that. I had no idea."

"She was there one moment, and the next she was gone."

"And you were in the mine when it happened?" Isaac clarified before taking a sip of his sweet tea.

"Yes, I found a clue that I wanted to look into," Piper said. "Luna—she's my intern—and I were taking pictures and totally distracted. I had no idea Julie might be in danger while we were doing so."

"That is eerie that you guys were so close when she disappeared." Isaac shook his head as he stared into the distance, his eyes far off in thought. "Did you tell anybody what you were doing? Where you were going?"

"No, I didn't. It was supposed to be a simple day trip to see if my hunch was right. If I discovered anything, then I was going to turn those findings over to law enforcement. I had no idea that danger would be waiting, or I would have never taken Julie and Luna with me into the mine . . ." Piper's voice trailed with regret.

"I'm so sorry, Piper." Madison squeezed her hand. "I wish there was something I could tell you or do . . ."

Piper absently rubbed the side of her glass. "Me too. I feel like I shouldn't be here right now in the comfort of this house with warm food and water, especially since I have no idea what Julie might be going through." A tear trickled down her cheek.

Bear squeezed Piper's arm, wishing he could do more to comfort her. But there was no way to make her feel better.

Piper simply had to get through this.

He prayed there would be a happy ending waiting on the other side. But he had firsthand experience that happy endings weren't guaranteed.

———

Isaac and Madison left an hour later. The two of them were staying at their childhood cabin and trying to fix it up. At least, that was what Piper had picked up on from the conversation she'd heard.

That meant it was just Piper and Bear here right now. In some circumstances, Piper would be unnerved at that thought. Staying with a strange man out in the middle of nowhere? It wasn't exactly on her bucket list.

But she had a gut feeling about Bear. Although she didn't know him well, she sensed that he was trustworthy and a gentleman. She felt safe with him, and she'd much rather be here than at a hotel.

Eight months ago, they'd connected online. A couple of weeks afterward, Bear had attended one of her lectures. They'd eventually struck up a friendship.

Last month, Bear had asked Piper to examine some of the video footage left by the GSK.

She'd been more than happy to help.

If Bear knew about the ordeal back in Chicago, he didn't say anything.

He hadn't run. He'd never made her feel judged or incompetent.

With any luck, she'd only be staying here one night. Maybe tomorrow, they would have some answers.

Piper stood by the window and stared outside at the darkness.

Julie was out there somewhere. Piper wished it was her instead. She wished she was the one who'd been taken.

Her assistant hadn't asked to be involved in any of this. She was innocent and kind and sweet. Piper was the driven one. That very drive often helped her find answers—but it had also gotten her in trouble on more than one occasion.

Piper felt Bear behind her. She was all too aware of his presence. Too aware—aware as in every fiber of her being seemed to come alive when he was near.

She needed to put an end to that. Because even if she could trust the man, she needed to keep her distance. Teamwork wasn't exactly her thing anymore—not now that she'd been burned.

"You doing okay?" Bear asked quietly, almost as if trying to get a read on her current mental state.

She shrugged, knowing better than to give a flippant answer. "As well as I can be considering my friend is missing and someone associated with the GSK took her."

"Our theory was right. Ralph Burgess had an understudy working for him."

"This is one time I wish I wasn't right." Heaviness pressed on her chest.

As an eerie feeling washed over her, Piper dropped the curtain and took a step back.

"What is it?" Bear peered out the window as if looking for the source of her distress.

"Just an uncomfortable feeling." She rubbed her arms, suddenly chilled. "Like someone was watching me or something."

Bear studied her a moment before gazing out the window again. "Do you think that guy's out there?"

"I don't know." Piper shook her head a little too quickly and suddenly felt off-balance. "It could be my emotions playing with me. But I don't think we should stand here and give any unseen eyes the chance to observe what we're doing right now, just in case."

He stared outside one more time before closing the curtains and taking her elbow to lead her away.

"I know you must be exhausted," he murmured. "Don't you want to get some sleep?"

Piper shook her head. "I don't think I could sleep if I tried. Doing anything that brings me comfort also brings me a wave of guilt."

"How about if you and I talk about what's going on and see if we can figure out some answers? Tomorrow's a new day, I don't have any classes scheduled. I'm more than happy to do whatever is necessary to help you find your friend."

Gratitude washed through her. "Thank you. I would love to sit down and try to hammer some ideas out."

"Then let's get busy."

Those words were music to her ears.

At least, she'd be doing *something* . . .

CHAPTER
EIGHT

BEAR AND PIPER sat at his kitchen table, coffee in front of them as well as some chocolate-covered peanuts he'd picked up from his favorite farmers market in the fall.

Now that they'd settled in, it was time to get down to business.

He studied Piper's face as he tried to think through how to proceed. "Do we want to start with our plans for tomorrow? Or do you want to start by revisiting the past?"

Piper pushed a stray lock of hair that had fallen out of her stubby ponytail behind her ear. "Actually, I've already set up a meeting tomorrow with someone who used to mine those tunnels."

Bear's eyebrows shot up. "When did you do that?"

"While you, your brother, and sister were talking, I did some research on my phone and found someone local—Rex Morgan—who used to work for North Elk Ridge. On a whim, I sent an email, and *bam*! He responded a few minutes later, and now I'm taking him to lunch. Do you want to come?"

Bear would be lying if he said he wasn't impressed. "Absolutely. You've always been a go-getter, haven't you?"

"I've been called that—and I've been called worse. Much worse." A frown tugged at her lips.

He stared at Piper a moment, wondering exactly what she was getting at. Of course, he knew about the scandal surrounding her. He knew there could be more to the story, but Piper would share those details if she wanted to.

In the meantime, he reminded himself again to keep his distance.

"Okay, since you already have that meeting set up, then how about we revisit the past a bit?" He grabbed a notebook from a shelf at the end of the kitchen island. "I think we should jot down the suspects in this case. Why don't we start there?"

"Right. So far, there's Arnie Siebert, Ted Russo, and Harry Simpkins." Piper named them as quickly as other people might name the months of the year.

"Impressive. But some of those guys were cleared."

"Here's where it gets tricky," Piper reminded him. "Sure, most of these men had an alibi for some of these murders. But what people weren't considering back then was the fact that more than one person could be involved. That means any of these guys' alibis could be null and void, right?"

"I guess you're right. But we don't want to go around accusing people unjustly. I know what that's like."

She offered a compassionate smile. "I know. I can't even imagine what you've been through with your father, and you're right—that's the last thing we want to do. But not all hope is lost."

"What do you mean?"

"I think I found a way to separate which guy murdered who." Her voice lilted as if the possibility excited her.

"You mean, based on the hands? Because in some of the videos the killer was wearing gloves so . . ."

"Yes, there's that. But I really feel like this second killer is much more clever than the first. Ralph Burgess was playing games with everyone. He's definitely brilliant in a very twisted, sadistic way. But this second guy thinks he's smarter than everybody else, and he left subtle clues at the crime scenes as well as in some of his videos."

Bear locked his gaze with Piper's. "I would love for you to explain to me exactly what you're thinking right now."

A mixture of excitement and wariness danced in her eyes. "I'd be more than happy to. But just take everything with a grain of salt."

———

Piper had gone over the other objects of interest she'd found in the crime-scene photos.

One was the compact disc that had been in the CD player when Lisa Moreno was electrocuted in her pool. A Third Eye Blind CD was inside, homemade, with only one song on it—"Never Let You Go."

From what Piper had gathered, Lisa had never really been a fan of the music group.

After she reviewed those possible clues, she and Bear added to the list of suspects and made notes.

Arnie Siebert—a local wedding and party emcee. He'd been a news anchor before being fired for sexual harassment. His dad was a doctor.

Ted Russo—Head of Parks and Rec in Fog Lake for more than twenty years. Found on side of road helping a woman who'd been hit by a car. Was wearing a Go-Pro.

Harry Simpkins—colleague of Bear's dad, James Colson, at the local high school. Would have known enough about James to make the man look guilty.

Rod Wilkins—social worker who was there when Bear, Isaac, and Madison were taken into custody. Gives off weird vibes. Helped look for two missing people abducted by the GSK in January.

Kevin Black—dated Lisa Moreno. Just came back into town four months ago. Works at an electronics store, so he knows technology.

Skip Johnson—former prisoner who was just released on parole last month. He went to prison around the time of what was thought to be the last GSK murder fifteen years ago.

Leonard Kincy—owned an auto repair shop in Fog Lake. Known as a troublemaker around town. Was seen with one of the victims before she died.

"They're all fair game again as far as I'm concerned." Piper pushed the paper toward Bear and leaned back in her chair to let her thoughts simmer a moment.

"It will be practically impossible to check these guys' alibis from nearly twenty years ago," Bear said. "But we *can* check their alibis for the time Julie was abducted."

"Absolutely." They were both on the same page.

Bear leaned closer, his gaze locking with hers. "I have to warn you that none of these guys will take kindly to us asking around about them. I'm sure the FBI is looking into everyone they can think of."

"I'm sure they are." Piper tapped her pen against the paper. "We can also narrow this down based on who had a connection with Ralph Burgess."

Bear tilted his head, showing his doubt. "Ralph was smart. I'm sure if he had someone working with him, it's not going to be obvious the two were connected."

Piper frowned as she chewed on his words. "You're right. It sounds like we have quite the job in front of us."

Their gazes locked. "Maybe those crime-scene photos will continue to speak to you."

"We can only hope," Piper muttered.

Just then, her phone buzzed. She clicked on the text message from the unknown number and discovered someone had sent her an audio text.

After a second of hesitation, she put the phone on speaker and hit Play.

A computer-animated voice filled the air, almost sounding singsongy.

"You'll never find her. You'll never find her. You'll never find her."

The message was followed by evil laughter that made Piper's blood go cold.

CHAPTER
NINE

THERE'S MORE than one way to get somewhere.

Most people go the easiest route from Point A to Point B. But there are other ways than the expected ones.

You can also go under and through, which makes entirely more sense sometimes—especially if you know what you're doing.

Under and through were filled with uncertainties. But darkness doesn't always have to be scary. In fact, I've come to quite enjoy it.

I look in the mirror and sigh. I can't miss work today. My absence would be too suspicious. Word is spreading all over Fog Lake about the missing woman.

Her parents had called the media, and reporters

were beginning to flood into town. Everywhere I went last night, I saw news vans and reporters.

I left her somewhere safe, somewhere she wouldn't be found.

I was going to kill her yesterday right after I grabbed her. I had a whole scenario set up in my mind—a scenario involving her being lost in an old mine. I would rescue her.

At first.

And then . . .

I smile.

However, I decided to wait. I have my reasons—good reasons.

For instance, Julie knows Piper Stephens. They worked together. That means, Julie should know everything Piper has discovered.

I simply need to get Julie to talk and spill everything she knows.

In the meantime, not all hope is lost.

Those bodies that were discovered? I've been working on my stockpile for years. I always picked the unknowns to be my secret, unbroadcasted victims. That's why I've been able to keep my hobby quiet for so long.

But no more.

The attention this discovery is getting makes me

feel emboldened—even though no one knows I'm responsible. Still, I feel powerful that I've had this stronghold over people for so long.

They're so oblivious. Simply *clueless*.

I glance at my computer, at the secret account I set up on the dark web. No one will discover me there. I'm smarter than people give me credit for.

I'm even smarter than Bear Colson. He's supposed to be an expert. He teaches classes. Trains a new generation of law enforcement. He's even consulted with the FBI on a few cases, from what I've heard.

But he knows nothing.

That's because I've always insisted on going under and through instead of over. I've chosen the dark recesses instead of the easy route.

I watch the video one more time before pressing Send.

Then I wait.

It will take some time, but eventually the FBI will discover the footage.

They'll know there's another body.

They'll scramble to find it.

Delight begins to fill me.

Then my brow furrows as another thought butts in.

What if Piper Stephens gets in my way?

I fear she knows too much already.

And, if that's the case, then I'll need to silence her.

Grabbing her might prove to be difficult.

But I've always been up for a good challenge.

CHAPTER
TEN

BEAR'S MIND had raced all night as he reviewed what he'd learned the day before. At the moment, before the sun even rose, he lay in his bed, unable to sleep as he thought things through.

He'd known that Piper was brilliant.

But she was proving that fact again and again.

Every time he closed his eyes, he remembered Piper's intelligent gaze. Her pert features. Her petite figure.

It had been a long time since he'd had feelings for anyone.

Not since Sasha had broken his heart and reminded Bear why being alone was so appealing. But being around Piper . . .

Her presence revitalized something inside him

and made him feel an excitement he hadn't experienced in years.

But Bear needed to remind himself to stay in check.

Piper wouldn't be staying long. Besides, the woman was going through a crisis right now. Bear hoped the situation wouldn't end with trauma.

More than anything, he wanted Julie to be found and for this whole serial killer saga to be put to rest once and for all. It had been going on for far too long now.

His father had been imprisoned fifteen years for crimes he didn't commit. *Fifteen years.*

The real killer's spree had begun four years before that.

Nearly two decades of fear surrounded this town and the people living here.

That thought ignited a passion for justice inside Bear. People should be able to live with more peace of mind. Ninety-eight percent of the people in this area were good, hardworking folk. It was a shame that such a small percentage had to ruin it for everyone else.

But Bear had learned that was simply life.

At 5:30 a.m., he finally hopped out of bed and worked out. Afterward, he fed his chickens and gathered fresh eggs, showered, and got ready for the day before heading downstairs to make breakfast.

Cooking had become a hobby for him. The interest hadn't begun until after he'd started his own garden, which had then led to canning, which had led to practically a mini farm here on this property. He had twenty-two chickens and had plans to add some goats in the spring.

Now that he'd experienced living this way, he couldn't imagine doing anything else.

When he wasn't working or taking care of his land, he'd also taken up the hobby of creating custom knives. One side of his garage had been set up as a gym and the other held his welding equipment. He sold the pieces online, but he hadn't been working on them as much lately.

Too many things in his life had distracted him.

Just as he'd prepped everything to make omelets, Piper came down the steps.

Bear sucked in a breath at the sight of her.

Even in her well-worn jeans and sweatshirt, she was still one of the most beautiful women he'd ever seen—and fascinating. He wanted to know more about her, more about what had led her to this point in her life, what her life was like back in Lexington, what her plans for the future were.

She smiled almost shyly at him—and shy was not something that fit Piper Stephens.

"I thought I heard someone down here." She paused on the other side of the breakfast bar and observed him as he stood behind the griddle.

"I thought we should both eat before we head out." He poured her a cup of coffee—black, just as she'd requested yesterday—and handed it to her. "We'll need to keep our energy up."

"Breakfast sounds good. I'm hungrier than I realized." She raised her mug. "And thanks for this."

Bear had noticed she didn't eat much soup last night. Considering the circumstances, he couldn't blame her. Still, the woman was thin enough that she shouldn't miss too many meals.

"What do you like in your omelet?" he asked.

She glanced at the bowls he had set up in front of him. "Cheese, sausage, and onions sound great."

"Coming right up." He poured some fresh eggs he'd beaten onto the griddle and listened to them sizzle. "Turkey sausage okay?"

"Sure. You like to eat healthy, huh?"

"I have something called alpha-gal. It was caused by a Lone Star tick bite, and it means I can't have any red meat or dairy products."

Her eyes widened. "I've heard about that. How did you figure out you had it?"

"I ordered a steak at a restaurant, and my throat started closing up," Bear said. "I was rushed to the hospital and—after an encounter with an EpiPen—they tested me and told me about alpha-gal. I hadn't heard of it before. Now, it's changed my whole life."

"That's crazy."

"Tell me about it. But I'm thankful that I don't have it as bad as some people. One man I met said he can't even be around red meat as it's being grilled. Just the smoke coming off it causes his windpipe to constrict."

"I can't even imagine." Piper glanced at the food he'd assembled. "Can I do anything to help?"

"You just sit there and take it easy."

She took a sip of her coffee and leaned back. "I don't suppose you've heard anything else since we talked last night?"

Bear shook his head before adding the fillings to Piper's omelet. "Even if the FBI has discovered anything else, I'm sure we won't hear for a while."

Piper frowned and nodded slowly. "That's what I thought too. But I guess I was hoping . . ."

"I know you're thinking about your friend." He glanced at her face, looking for a sign of how she was really doing. "I've been thinking about her also."

"I can't get Julie out of my mind." Piper let out a

soft breath. "I checked my computer before I came down, but I didn't see any new videos."

"That's a good thing, right?"

"It could be. But it doesn't fit this guy's MO. He never keeps his victims alive. He 'saves' them and then kills—" Her voice cracked as she seemed to realize what she'd said. She rubbed her throat and stared into her coffee, clearly unable to finish.

Bear cleared his throat, unsure how much he should say. But Piper deserved to know the truth. She'd helped him out, and now it was his turn to return the favor.

"What is it?" Piper studied his face, not daring to look away as if that might give him a chance to deny what she saw.

"There actually *was* one victim who got away." Bear folded the omelet over. "Her story hasn't been made public yet—she wants to keep her privacy."

"What?" Piper's voice climbed with curiosity. "There is a survivor?"

Bear nodded, almost feeling somber.

"Can you tell me more?" She leaned toward Bear, propping her elbows on the table, her attention totally and completely on him.

He plated her omelet and let out a breath as he contemplated what to say. "Just between you and me, the crime happened about nine years ago. The

GSK put this woman in a pit and kept her for about eight hours before deciding to let her go. She didn't report what happened until recently, however. She's one of the reasons we were able to catch the real Good Samaritan Killer last month."

"I can't believe I didn't hear about that," Piper murmured, not touching her omelet.

"Like I said, it's a matter of privacy. It's not my story to tell."

Piper's gaze made it obvious her mind was racing at a million miles a minute. "But the fact that there was a victim who survived changes things. Any time a criminal changes his MO—"

"That signals a change in their life usually."

Piper stared at Bear a moment as if impressed.

"That's right." Piper nibbled on her lip a moment. "So, something has changed. What is it about Julie that would make this guy keep her alive? Not that I am complaining. I want her alive. I want to find her and hug her and spend the rest of my life apologizing to her and—"

"I have a theory." Bear poured more eggs on the griddle and studied them a minute as he gathered his thoughts.

He knew Piper wouldn't like what he had to say. But withholding the truth from her also felt wrong.

"What is it?" she rushed.

He sucked in a deep breath before starting.

———

Piper could hardly breathe as she waited to hear what Bear had to say. Whatever it was, she had a feeling it was big. Maybe even life-changing.

"In all these years, you're the only one who ever thought anything about that map in the crime-scene photo," Bear started as he sprinkled some green onions on his eggs. "You're the only one who thought to go up to that mine to look for possible evidence."

"Okay . . ."

"And Julie was your assistant. That means that she's privy to what you discovered and what you know, right?"

Piper's head swam.

She knew where Bear was going with this, but she wasn't ready to come to that conclusion herself. He was going to have to say the words aloud. Otherwise, she'd stay in denial.

"Right . . ." Her voice sounded strained.

"Then this guy might be trying to figure out what else you know. If you figured out the mine, then maybe he thinks you figured out other things. And if you've figured out other things, then maybe eventually you're going to figure out who he is, and his power trip will be over."

Piper swallowed hard as she used her fork to cut into her omelet. "But this guy thinks he's smarter than everyone else. He's probably not going to give me that much credit."

"I don't doubt for a moment that this discovery has shaken him up. It's caused him to break out of his normal routine."

"Which may explain why there's no video yet."

"Exactly." Bear's gaze latched onto hers. "Is there anything Julie might say that could give him the upper hand? Will she talk?"

Piper lowered her fork before she even tried her omelet. "I hate to say it, but I hope she does. The thought of that man hurting her in order to get information about me? It's not okay."

Bear placed his own omelet on a plate. "I know it's not. That's why I hesitated to bring it up."

"No, you were right to do so. I just can't stand the thought of something happening to someone because of me."

"That just makes you a good person."

She let out a breath and stared off in the distance. After Bear had gone through all this hard work to make her breakfast, she didn't want to tell him that she'd lost her appetite. She would try to force down what she could.

Piper had to find her friend. She had no other choice.

She'd figure out a plan if it was the last thing she did.

PIPER FELT a rush of nerves as she and Bear stepped into the Hometown Diner four hours later.

After breakfast, she and Bear had picked up her car. She had an overnight bag in the trunk, leftover from a trip to see her brother in Louisville a couple of days ago, along with her laptop.

At the time, she'd scolded herself for being unorganized. But now, leaving the bag there seemed fortuitus. It certainly beat driving back to Lexington to pick up her things or buying new clothes.

With any luck, she'd be heading back home soon. Julie would be found, and this nightmare would be over.

When Piper and Bear got back to his place, they sat down to examine more videos, to look at maps of the area, to brainstorm people Ralph Burgess had possibly known.

They'd made a list of traits this guy would need to have: Medical knowledge to first save his victims before killing them. He was probably ordinary-looking, so he'd blend in. Perhaps he even seemed trustworthy. Somehow, he had to be connected to Ralph Burgess. He had to be tech savvy and to have been in town years ago.

Their list didn't necessarily rule anyone out.

The problem was that Ralph had been a politician, so he knew a lot of people. Plus, there was little possibility she'd be able to talk to the man since he was being held in custody while awaiting trial.

Her best bet would be to talk to his wife, Anita, or his son, Anthony. But she doubted either of them would want to talk to her. Bear said he might be able to arrange something, but he sounded doubtful.

She scanned the diner with its sit-down counter stretching across the back wall and glittery booths on a black-and-white-checked floor. The place was nostalgically outdated, but the owners played that up to their advantage. The oldies music playing from the jukebox was the icing on the cake. Currently, "My Girl" crooned through the speakers.

Her gaze stopped on Rex Morgan. Piper had found his picture on social media so she could identify him. The man was in his late sixties, with a square face, thinning hair, and a quick smile. He wore a red-and-blue plaid shirt with a windbreaker jacket and work boots.

He sat in a corner booth with what looked like sweet tea in front of him.

Piper offered a friendly smile and headed his way, Bear beside her.

She couldn't help but notice the glances Bear got as he walked through the restaurant.

Was that because he was a Colson and his father had been convicted as a serial killer? Or was it because of his imposing size and striking good looks?

Piper wasn't sure. It could be both.

She slid into the booth, and Bear sat beside her. She flashed another grateful smile at Rex. "Thank you so much for agreeing to meet with us."

"No problem." He readjusted his hat, almost as if he wanted to tip it toward her. "I'm happy to help however I can. You say you want to know about the mines?"

She nodded. "How about if you order some food first? Lunch is on me."

Piper wanted more than anything just to dive into the conversation. But she also didn't want to be repeatedly interrupted.

A few minutes later, all three of them had placed

their orders. Piper knew she should probably get a salad or something semi-healthy, but the smell of grilled meat and deep-fried potatoes got the best of her. She ordered a cheeseburger and fries instead.

When the waitress was gone, she turned back to Rex. "How long did you work at North Elk Ridge Mine?"

He played with the edge of the napkin beneath his glass of tea as he answered. "I got a job there when I was eighteen. I worked there for thirty years until they shut down. Then I started working at one of the warehouses owned by Mick Moreno."

"What did you do at the mines?" Bear asked.

"By the time it shut down, I was a supervisor. Made sure no one got hurt and that everyone did their job. My record was unblemished, so I'd say I was pretty good at what I did." He let out a wheezy chuckle.

"We know that the main entrance to the mine is pretty grandiose," Piper said. "But can you tell me what it's like inside? I'm assuming it's not just one or two straight tunnels through the mountain."

"Oh, no. It's definitely not." Rex's expression turned animated. "Think of the place like the roots of a tree. That's what the system is like."

Piper shivered at the thought of it. If that was true, then there were all kinds of places a person could get lost—or hide in, hoping to never be discovered.

"I didn't realize it was that extensive." Piper had looked online trying to find out more information. But thirty years ago, the internet wasn't what it was today—it was just in its infancy, really.

"It wasn't safe. There were toxic fumes, deadly gases, coal dust, fatal lung disease. That's just to start." Rex adjusted his hat again. "I hated working at that place. I have a bit of claustrophobia, truth be known."

"Then it doesn't sound like the job was an ideal fit," Piper muttered.

"Not at all." Rex let out a little laugh. "Back then, working at the mine was one of the only ways to make a living in this area. You did what you had to do. I was married at seventeen, and I had a family to support. People didn't mind working back in the day."

"I understand," Piper said. "I have family in West Virginia, and they would say the same thing."

"Out by Beckley?"

She nodded. "As a matter of fact, yes."

The waitress delivered their food.

Piper lifted a quick prayer before turning back to Rex.

This conversation had been pleasant so far. But

she really needed to dig into some deeper details if she was going to find any answers . . . and if she wanted to find Julie.

———————

"So, could you tell us more about North Elk Ridge Mine?" Bear asked as he ate his grilled chicken, steamed vegetables, and potatoes.

"The whole system is crazy." Rex picked up a fry. "I don't remember exactly how many miles under-ground it runs, but it was like a never-ending labyrinth. Once, John Rankins got drunk and wandered into the mine after hours. He got lost there for five days before anyone found him. I'm amazed he didn't run out of oxygen, truth be told."

"What about entrances?" Piper asked. "Is there anywhere else you can enter the mine?"

"We call those openings portals. And, yes, there are several places. Most people don't know about them, though."

Piper sucked in a breath beside him. "Like where?"

"There are various shaft entrances all throughout that mountain. Which one do you want to know about?"

"Are there any close to town?" Piper asked before taking a bite of her burger.

Rex tapped his finger against his chin as he thought about it. "There's one behind Falling Timbers, the camp store that Boone Wilder owns. It's probably about a quarter mile away. If I had to guess, that's the closest one to town."

Piper and Bear exchanged a glance. It was worth checking out.

"Do you think someone could maneuver inside one of these smaller shafts without getting lost?" Piper asked.

Rex grunted. "That's a tough one. Maybe if someone found an old map that detailed the space, they could."

"Any idea where someone might find one of these old maps?" Piper asked. "Do any of the bigwigs from the mine still live around here?"

"Last time I heard, most of them left when the mine shut down, even OJ Deerman."

"OJ?" Bear asked.

"He owned the mine. Seemed like a nice enough man. But money was his bottom line. When the mine closed, he and his brother moved on to other ventures. Couldn't tell you what."

"His brother?" Bear clarified, trying to take in as much information as he could.

"Yeah, OD. Funny, huh? OJ and OD?" Rex let out a chuckle. "Anyway, OD is OJ's half-brother. The two were characters—got along like cats and dogs. OJ was the serious, exacting one. OD was more laid-back and likeable. I remember hearing stories about those two . . ."

"They could be a good source for us to talk to about the mines," Piper said.

"Probably. But they've been gone from around here for a long time. Not sure where they went, truthfully. Probably looking for other ways to get rich. Although, OJ would have to be in his eighties . . ."

"And OD?" Bear asked.

Rex sighed. "He was a bit younger. Maybe twenty years younger, even. I haven't heard anything about him in years. My guess is he went off and retired somewhere. He didn't have roots here, so there was no reason to stay."

"Who owns the mines now?" Piper asked.

Rex shrugged. "I suppose the government took them over."

Several minutes later, they finished their food, and Piper paid. Bear thought about offering to take the bill, but this was her gig. He didn't think Piper would accept his offer, and he didn't want to make the situation awkward.

As they left the restaurant, Piper shifted closer to him. "I want to see the different mineshafts."

"I don't think that's a good idea." Tension threaded across Bear's back at the thought of all the trouble she could get into.

She paused in front of him. "I didn't say I wanted to go inside to walk around or explore. I just want to know what these entrances look like. I need to see them so I can picture what may have played out—to see if it's a possibility the killer may have gotten inside in time to grab Julie."

Bear gave her another look.

Piper was a visual person, he reminded himself. That was why she took pictures. Seeing things was how she processed information.

He knew he couldn't talk her out of going to see the entrance behind the camp store. If he didn't go with her then she'd simply go alone. It was better if Bear accompanied her so he could talk her out of any bad ideas.

"Let's go." He nodded toward his truck.

Piper didn't bother to hide the relief on her face. "Perfect. Because I really didn't want to go alone."

CHAPTER
TWELVE

AS PIPER and Bear walked to his truck, his phone rang. From what Piper gathered, it was Special Agent Townsend, or Shane, as Bear called him.

Bear muttered several things into the phone before ending the call and turning toward her. "Shane wants to know if we can head to the sheriff's office for a moment. It's just down the street. He has an update for us."

"Of course." Piper pulled her knit cap down farther over her ears to keep them warm before tucking her hands into her jacket pockets.

There was certainly a nip in the air today. But that only made this mountain town seem even more beautiful.

Piper had never been to Fog Lake before, and the

place was charming, like a more downhome version of Gatlinburg. The town with its quaint shops boasted a square in the center and inviting seasonal decorations on every corner. At this time of the year, the decorations were mostly snowmen, which provided perfect photo ops for tourists.

Snow-dusted mountains surrounded the place, but the lake at the center of town stole the show. Even now, a thick mist hung over its gray, winter-garnished water.

"This seems like a great place to live," Piper told Bear as they walked. "I mean, aside from all the murders."

She hadn't meant for her words to be humorous, and she hoped she didn't sound glib about tragedy. The staggering contrast couldn't be ignored, however.

"Things you never thought you would say, huh?" Bear cast her a knowing glance.

"Yes, kind of. The whole place seems so idyllic. Yet things aren't always as they seem, are they?" Piper shoved her hands farther into her pockets as the cold nipped at her.

"I'm sure you know about the town's history. Some people believe it's cursed, that the blood of our ancestors and the spirits of those who were massacred still haunt this area."

Piper had heard the stories about the Native American massacre that happened here more than two hundred years ago. It was tragic, to say the least. "And what do you think?"

He shrugged. "I've never believed in ghosts. But I do believe that past mistakes can play a role in present circumstances."

Piper shivered just at the thought of it. She didn't believe in ghosts either, even though one of her former colleagues had repeatedly claimed that he'd photographed orbs in some nighttime photos. She didn't buy it.

They continued walking until they reached the sheriff's office. Multiple news vans were parked outside, and several reporters and cameramen gathered near the door.

Piper and Bear quickly walked past, and Bear held open the door to usher her inside. Piper hurried by, not wanting any unnecessary attention. Before they even reached the receptionist, Townsend appeared and directed them into a conference room.

The agent shut the door behind them, offered them coffee, which they refused, and then they all sat at a large table. "Thanks for coming."

"I take it something happened." Nerves spread their uneasiness through Piper's limbs.

Townsend had called them here to share an update. Had they found Julie? Was she okay?

Piper swallowed hard, trying to push down those nerves.

"We IDed one of the victims we found in the mine." Townsend's expression remained grim.

One of the victims? Not Julie?

Piper felt her shoulders slump as a whoosh of relief swept through her.

"We don't usually share sensitive information like this," Townsend continued. "But, Bear, since you have been a part of this investigation from the beginning, I thought you'd want to know."

"I appreciate it."

"And, Piper, since you're the one who found the information leading to the discovery, I wanted to include you also." His gaze locked on hers. "But what I tell you doesn't leave this room. We haven't released this information to the media yet. We still need to get in touch with family members."

"Understood," Piper muttered.

"What was the victim's name?" Bear asked.

Townsend let out a breath before pulling up a photo on his phone. The woman there had light-brown hair past her shoulders, a defiant gaze, and multiple piercings in her ears.

"Fiona Davis," Townsend said. "She grew up in

Maryville but ran away from home several years ago. She was last seen in Gatlinburg, where she'd found a waitressing job and was looking for a permanent place to stay."

"What else can you tell us about her?" Piper asked, still staring at the woman's photo.

"Fiona was twenty-three. She had a rough background. A bad family life. Nothing really to tie her to the area where she grew up. From what I heard, she was pretty brash and not liked by very many people."

"When was she last seen?" Bear asked.

"Four years ago."

Piper closed her eyes.

These weren't old bones. Not relatively speaking, at least. This guy had continued his killing spree, only he'd hid the evidence.

A change in MO.

Which would indicate that something had also changed in his life, just like she and Bear talked about earlier.

"How many other bodies were there?" Bear asked.

Townsend rubbed his jaw and tilted his head slightly as if he didn't want to acknowledge the truth. But finally, he said, "Five. There are at least five others."

Piper's head spun.

This went much deeper than she'd ever imagined.

———

Bear sensed Piper's apprehension, and he couldn't blame her.

This whole investigation just kept getting stranger and stranger.

But as they climbed into his truck, Piper's laser focus returned. "I still want to see the mine entrances. I need to know what's possible. And unless I see it for myself . . . I don't know if I'll truly understand it."

"Then let's go."

He started his truck and only let it heat a few minutes before heading toward Falling Timbers Camping and General Store. Just as they were about to pull into the parking lot, a car came barreling down the road toward them.

Bear swerved into the lot to avoid being hit. Just as he did, the other driver jerked back into his own lane.

"Was that . . . ?" Bear craned his neck.

"Who?"

Bear frowned. "Arnie Siebert."

"Arnie the emcee?" Piper asked. "One of our suspects? Are you sure that was him?"

"I'm nearly certain. Although, the only thing nearby are some campgrounds. Arnie doesn't strike me as the outdoorsy type."

What if he had been at the mine entrance? Was that too much of a stretch?

He wasn't sure, but he stored that theory in the back of his mind.

Bear pulled into a parking space and glanced over at Falling Timbers. The place was located off the side of the road. In warmer weather, the store was hopping with fishermen, hikers, campers, whitewater rafters, and other kinds of adventure seekers.

Boone Wilder—Sheriff Wilder's younger brother —owned the place. Boone and Bear had talked on occasion about various hikes in the area. The man was easy to talk to and knowledgeable. Boone had always been kind, even when almost everyone else in town had turned their backs on Bear and his family.

As soon as Bear walked inside, he called hello to Boone and his employee, Chigger Wati. Chigger was a staple in Fog Lake with his infectious laughter and friendly manner. Bear quickly introduced Piper to them.

"What brings you two by?" Boone paused in front of them, a cardboard box of tackle at his feet. He wore his typical outdoors gear—a thermal shirt, a puffy green vest, and a knit hat on his head.

"We heard there's a mineshaft close by," Piper told him before Bear could answer.

Bear's eyebrows flickered up, but he decided to let her take the lead. This was her thing anyway.

"The mineshaft?" Boone paused with a bright-green wobbler in his hand. "This wouldn't by chance have something to do with yesterday's discovery, would it?"

Piper opened her mouth but shut it again.

Bear stepped closer. "Piper is actually the one who made the discovery. She's a forensic specialist, so she's trying to piece together a few things in her mind."

Boone studied her a moment before nodding. "There is an old mineshaft opening not too far from here."

"Can you tell us how to get to it?" Piper's voice contained a touch of eager determination.

Boone slid the lure onto the rack in front of him before turning to give Bear and Piper his full attention. "I can. But I need to warn you to be careful. Not many people know these shafts are there, and that's for a reason. All we need around here are some bored teenagers discovering them and deciding to get into some trouble—trouble that could lead to serious bodily injury or death."

"I don't want trouble," Piper told him. "I just need to see it with my own eyes. I'm trying to put the pieces together, and it's important that I visualize it."

After another moment of contemplation, Boone finally nodded and gave them directions.

"It's not going to be an easy hike," he warned. "Especially with the patchy snow. You'll have to cross the stream as well. In the summer, it's easy. But, in conditions like this, I'm sure I don't need to tell you that you don't want to fall in."

"Isn't there a footbridge?" Bear asked.

"There is, but it's probably a quarter mile farther up the road." Boone shrugged. "So, it just depends on exactly what you're looking to do."

"We'll figure that out." Bear shifted. "Speaking of which, has anyone else come in here asking about it?"

Boone shook his head. "No, I can't say they have. Most of the time, I deny I know where it is, just to keep people out of trouble."

"Probably a good idea," Bear said. "But we promise we'll behave."

"How about this?" Boone crossed his arms. "You guys go check things out. But before you head back, come check in with me. If I don't hear from you in a few hours, then I'm going to send out a search team for you."

"It's a deal." Bear appreciated that Boone was looking out for them. Because everyone needed someone to watch their back.

Even when you were six feet four and could bench press three fifty.

CHAPTER
THIRTEEN

"SO, what's it going to be?" Piper asked when she and Bear stepped outside of Falling Timbers. "Foot-bridge or stream?"

They started down a small path that ran from the store alongside the snow-laden stream. As they walked, she strapped her camera around her neck and snapped several pictures. The scenery was too pretty not to capture.

"The answer is clear to me," Bear said.

She stared at him a moment before nodding. "Me too. The stream."

"That actually wasn't what I was thinking."

"The footbridge will take too long."

"But it's safer," Bear reminded her.

"I can hop across some rocks without falling in." She shrugged as if it weren't a big deal.

"They're not just rocks—they're slippery rocks. And, if you miss a step, this whole adventure is over. Best-case scenario, you're wet, freezing cold, and need to change. Worst-case, you twist your ankle, and we have to wait for the rescue squad."

Piper frowned. When he worded it like that, the answer seemed obvious. But she didn't want to run out of daylight either. Besides, there were a million other things she wanted to get done today.

Julie was missing, and every minute counted.

"So . . ." Bear stared at her.

Piper let out a breath and shrugged. "So . . . crossing the stream it is."

Bear chuckled. "Not what I expected, but okay. If that's what you want—but don't say I didn't warn you."

They continued down the path. The ground was fairly level here and cleared of snow. But she knew this was the easy part.

She swallowed hard, hoping she wouldn't get more than she'd bargained for. She wasn't exactly graceful. She never made any athletic team she tried out for in high school. Instead, she'd settled for being yearbook editor.

Bear paused by a narrower area of the partially snow-covered stream. The determined rapids were victorious in several spots as they defied the ice and bounced over rocks.

"This will be the easiest place to cross," Bear announced.

Piper stared at the barely visible river stones, most of which were partly hidden beneath a blanket of white. Pushing aside her apprehension, she nodded. This had been her idea. She couldn't back out now.

"Okay. Let's do this."

Bear cast her another look before nodding. "I'll go first, in case you need help."

"I don't—"

He leveled his gaze with her. "Just let me help you to make me feel better, okay?"

She chuckled at the earnest expression on his face. "Okay, then."

Bear was a good sport. She'd give him that.

And he was still so surprising. Piper couldn't get over how his actual person was so different than the image she'd formed of him after chatting online.

A man with brains and brawn?

It was like he'd stepped out of her daydreams.

But relationships weren't something Piper was necessarily good at. She was better off focusing on her career. Sure, her occupation had let her down before. Not just let her down. It had dropped her, leaving her plunging to certain death.

But maybe there was a chance for redemption.

She prayed that was the case.

But so much of that rode on what happened while she was in Fog Lake. Right now Julie was a priority over her career.

Bear crossed several rocks, testing each one but keeping his balance. He made it look easy.

Then he held out his hand to her. "Your turn."

Piper stared at his hand, hesitating only a moment. Finally, she lunged toward the first rock, found her footing, then crossed to the next.

Once she had her balance, she reached for Bear's hand. His fingers clasped hers.

She ignored the jolt of electricity that rushed through her. He was only holding her hand out of necessity, she reminded herself.

"You've got this," he murmured.

But as she got closer to the middle of the stream, self-doubt seemed to pummel her.

Bear was right.

If she fell in this water, she'd have more to worry about than being cold.

She sucked in a deep breath. *Mind over matter. If you believe, you can achieve.*

Bear crossed to the next rock, this one dead center

of the stream. "This step is going to be tricky. The rock isn't level, so you're really going to have to watch how you land."

Piper nodded and carefully stretched her leg toward the rock he'd indicated. As her boot touched the stone, she hesitated before shifting her weight onto it.

Just as she did, her foot slid out from beneath her, and she felt herself tumbling toward the stream.

And she knew without a doubt that this truly had been a terrible idea.

———

Bear saw Piper begin to slip and quickly grabbed her arm.

He pulled her to her feet before the river could immerse her.

She stood there a moment, clutching him and appearing stunned at what had almost happened.

Finally, she looked up at him, and relief filled her gaze—along with a touch of sheepishness. She cleared her throat and pushed a hair behind her ear.

"Thank you," Piper muttered.

"Are you okay?" Bear studied her a moment, trying to get a read on her. "Did you get wet?"

She examined her hiking boots before shaking her head. "No, you caught me just in time."

"Good. No more almost accidents, okay?" He tilted his head as he waited for her response.

Piper absently rubbed the side of her face. "Got it."

She seemed more focused as they continued. Finally, they reached the opposite bank. Bear didn't let go of her hand until they had maneuvered over the rest of the river rock and were on solid ground.

He liked the feel of her hand in his. Still, he reluctantly let go and reminded himself to keep his distance.

He examined her once more before they continued toward the site. "You got this?"

Piper offered a tight smile. "Absolutely. Let's go."

Her words sounded confident, but her smile faltered. She didn't complain as they headed deeper into the woods.

"So how did you get into photography, Piper?" Maybe if Bear distracted her, she could shake her nerves.

"Pictures? I've always loved them. I got my first camera when I was only seven, and I was hooked. I took photos all the time."

"That's great," he told her. "What did you take pictures of? Flowers? Animals?"

"My neighbors." She flashed a smile. "I wish I was joking, but I knew something fishy was going on at their house, and I was determined to document it."

"So did you?"

She paused and snapped a picture of the stream between several snowy branches before turning back to Bear. "As a matter of fact, the mom and dad next door were eventually arrested for laundering money."

"Impressive."

Piper shrugged as if she wasn't as convinced. "My parents didn't think so. They threatened to take my camera away, actually."

"But then you followed your dreams and made a name for yourself. Certainly, they had to see that." He tested a few rocks before starting up a steeper part of the trail.

"Maybe. I really felt like I was living out my dreams—at least, I did until it all fell apart."

Bear was curious about what had happened, but he didn't want to ask, didn't want to unnecessarily dredge up bad memories.

"I couldn't tell that photo was altered," Piper offered.

He held out his hand again to help Piper maneuver a vertical section and waited to see if she'd offer more information.

"Honestly, I think I was set up, but I have no way of proving it."

"Who would have set you up?" Bear asked.

"If I had to guess? One of my colleagues. In fact, he spoke out against me, telling people that I loved attention and that was my motive to lie." She shook her head, tension stretching through her gaze.

"That really stinks, to say the least."

"Tell me about it." Piper grunted as she climbed another rock. "I lost everything, and Tim got the promotion we were both in line for."

Was that bitterness in her voice? Bear wasn't certain. But he wouldn't blame her if that was the case.

Piper pulled herself up to level ground, still breathing hard. "In the end, it's going to be a good thing. I'm going to make things right."

"How so?" Bear climbed behind her. He'd switched places. He wanted to be there to catch her just in case she fell.

"I'm going to prove my innocence. I'm going to prove I'm competent and that Tim actually altered that photo *after* I looked at the original. He's the only one I know with both the skills and the motive to make me look bad."

"Good for you." He admired her determination.

They climbed several more feet before Bear paused.

"Why are you stopping?" Piper looked back at him, breathing hard as she tried to catch her breath.

He nodded toward something in the distance. "Because we're at the mineshaft."

CHAPTER
FOURTEEN

PIPER STARED at the mine opening, her heart pounding against her ribcage.

So, *this* was what a shaft looked like.

The entire opening was probably only five by six, and metal-crossed lattice covered it. A padlock secured one side, making it clear someone could open this if necessary.

As Piper stood there, she felt cool air pouring out from the belly of the mountain, along with a dank, mineral-laden aroma.

She shivered.

"These openings are hidden all over the place, huh?" she muttered.

"That's what they say." Bear stared also.

"If someone had seen us approaching the mine on the hunting cameras yesterday, would it be possible for them to get into one of these, climb through the various tunnels, and somehow make it to the main tunnel in time to grab Julie?"

Bear peered through the grate and offered a half-shrug. "It seems like a long shot. It looks pretty steep."

Piper frowned as she gazed inside. "Maybe not all the shafts are like this. That theory is the only thing that makes sense to me. When someone grabbed Julie, he had to escape with her through a different exit. Either that, or this guy is keeping her somewhere in the mine system."

Bear squatted on the ground to examine something before pointing to an area in the dirt. "There are footprints here. They look fresh. There are two sets also—one larger than the other."

She sucked in a breath as they came into focus. One larger and one smaller? Like a man and a woman?

Her gaze swung toward the lock. Pulling her sleeve over her hand, she tugged at the metal clasp.

The lock slipped down, and she turned it, revealing the shackle wasn't locked in place.

"Someone may have done just what I suggested . . . from this very location," she muttered.

Bear stared at the padlock and let out a long

breath. "We need to report this to Shane . . . just to be on the safe side."

Piper nodded. "We most definitely do."

————

Bear and Piper hiked until they found phone service and then called Shane. He promised to send some men out.

In the meantime, Bear and Piper stuck around to make sure nothing happened to the clues they'd found. Piper had taken pictures to document everything as well.

Thankfully, Piper wasn't pushing hard to explore the shaft herself.

Finally, forty minutes later, two FBI agents and a park ranger arrived. Bear and Piper explained what they'd found, and then the agent in charge took over the scene.

"We should go," Bear gently told Piper. There was no reason to stay any longer—other than curiosity. But mostly, he and Piper would be in the way.

"What if Julie is in there—" Emotions clouded Piper's gaze.

"Then the FBI will find her." He kept his voice steady as he tried to reassure her. "They know what they're doing."

He placed his hand on Piper's back, directing her away from the scene. She glanced one more time at the shaft entrance but allowed him to guide her back the way they'd come. She was a smart lady. She had to know it wouldn't be wise for them to be out here after dark. In less than two hours, the sun would start to set.

They remained silent for several minutes until finally Piper asked, "So, you like to hike? I know I'm changing the subject, but I need to keep my mind occupied."

Bear welcomed the subject change also. "I do. I love being outside. I like the peace and solitude."

"Does that mean you go hiking alone?"

Memories tightened his throat. "Sometimes."

"Sometimes? It seems like a good date activity . . ." Piper outwardly cringed. "Sorry—that was not smooth at all. I guess I'm fishing to find out if you're seeing someone, and it just came out super awkward."

Bear let out a light laugh, trying to add some levity instead of showing his heartache. "I was dating someone for a while, but it didn't work out."

"Well, she was clearly a fool if she let you get away."

Why did Piper's affirmation fill him with a

moment of delight? "I appreciate the vote of confidence. Our lives just went in different directions."

"Did you meet her online?"

He cast Piper a sharp glance, and she shrugged.

"I just mean . . . you seem to like doing things online, so, in my mind, it just makes sense. Sorry if I'm prodding."

Talking to Piper about Sasha didn't seem as awkward as Bear would have assumed. He felt as if he'd known Piper for years instead of mere months.

"It's okay," Bear said. "No, we didn't meet online. We met while doing a hike about an hour from here. She's a travel blogger."

"Interesting."

"We started talking and discovered we had a lot in common. I volunteered to show her around the area, and she agreed. We were practically inseparable after that."

"It sounds like the two of you were a good match. I'm sorry it didn't work out."

"Everything works out in the end, right?" Bear said the words lightly, but the breakup had been a real turning point for him.

After Sasha, he'd withdrawn even more to himself.

Bear had been on the verge of proposing when Sasha's true colors were revealed.

She'd published several blog posts about Fog Lake—and she'd included information about Bear and the GSK.

She'd only been using him all along, wanting to hear his story to increase her popularity.

The memories still stung. For his entire life, people he'd loved had chosen other pursuits over him, starting with his dad. Bear didn't feel sorry for himself—but he did feel cautious.

How many more betrayals could he take before he closed himself off completely?

He glanced over and saw Piper starting down a particularly tricky section. She looked like an accident waiting to happen as she wobbled.

"Wait a second," he called. "Let me help. I'll go first."

Bear scrambled past her and down the six-foot section of stacked stones running alongside the stream. At the bottom, he offered his hand to steady her. "Just watch your footing."

"Will do." Piper placed her boot on one of the rocks that jutted out, an uncertain look on her face.

She wasn't the most athletic person, but she was surprisingly determined.

Just as she lowered her right foot, her left foot lost traction and she began to fall.

She let out a yelp as gravity pulled her downward toward the icy water.

Bear reached forward, his arms scooping beneath her legs and shoulders. He froze a moment to be sure they were stable.

They were.

Catastrophe averted.

Piper stared at him as he held her in his arms for longer than necessary.

"Thank you," she muttered, sounding breathless at their closeness.

Bear understood the feeling. "Any time."

He stared into her hazel eyes another moment before realizing he hadn't released her.

Clearing his throat, he set her on her feet.

Piper seemed just as flustered as Bear felt as she pushed hair out of her face and glanced up at him, something almost resembling shyness in her gaze. "It's a good thing you're here."

His blood grew warmer. "Yes, I guess it is."

Their gazes connected, and something passed between them—something strong that had been simmering ever since they met.

"Piper—"

Before he could finish, a stick cracked in the distance.

They both jerked their heads toward the sound, the moment between them broken.

Piper edged closer to him, a slight tremble claiming her voice. "What was that?"

Bear put a protective arm around her as he stared into the woods, worst-case scenarios rushing through his mind.

"I'm not sure," he finally said. "But we need to get moving—just in case."

CHAPTER
FIFTEEN

PIPER TRIED to get the noise in the woods out of her mind.

It was probably nothing. Just an animal.

Still, everything had her on edge lately.

As she hiked down the path, she tried to shift her thoughts to something more pleasant.

Like Bear.

What had passed between them earlier?

She kept mentally replaying Bear catching her as she fell.

He'd literally taken her breath away.

For a moment, all Piper had wanted to do was to reach up and touch his cheek. To feel the stubble beneath her fingers. To dream about what it would be like for his lips to touch hers.

But those were all foolish fantasies, the kind her

mother used to fuss at her for having. In fact, it was because of her mother she'd become a forensic photographer instead of just a regular photographer who booked family sessions and chased sunsets.

Her mother said Piper needed something less frivolous, something she could support herself with.

Her mom had been a 911 dispatcher, and her dad was an electrician. She'd lived a simple life growing up, but Piper's mom had felt strongly that Piper needed to know how to support herself.

As soon as all three kids had graduated from high school, her mom and dad had taken an early retirement and moved down to Florida where they could help take care of Piper's grandmother, who'd been battling cancer.

She and Bear continued down the trail. They hadn't heard any more sticks snap. Piper had to assume that it was probably just an animal.

But what if it wasn't?

A chill washed through her.

They bypassed crossing the stream and instead took the footbridge—just as they should have done the first time.

Finally, they were back at Falling Timbers and had gone inside to update Boone about what had happened.

"You found two sets of footprints?" Boone took a

long sip out of his thermos. "I tell you, I always had a bad feeling about those mines. I call them the Great Underground. In the wrong hands, those tunnels would be perfect for nefarious activities."

"I can see why," Piper said. "I just hope the FBI is able to figure out what's going on."

Boone leaned across the counter toward them. "Listen, I told my brother this also, but I'll mention it to the two of you. For years, Ted Russo has been pushing to do a mining exploration trip with some of the Explorer Cadet kids. He's shown an unusual interest in the place."

"You think because he knows something?" Bear asked.

Boone shrugged. "Your guess is as good as mine."

Julie's image filled Piper's mind again.

Piper *had* to find her friend. But every possible way to do that had led nowhere.

She frowned.

If the feds didn't find Julie soon, Piper would have to take desperate measures. She'd be left with no other choice.

————

As soon as Bear climbed into his truck, he cranked the engine, desperate for some warmth.

His mind still reeled after everything that had happened—and everything he'd learned—and he prayed the FBI would discover some answers soon.

The longer Julie was missing, the less likely authorities were to find her.

He wasn't sure how Piper would live with the guilt if something happened to her friend.

Piper pulled her collar closer around her neck as she glanced at him. "Thanks for coming along with me today. I appreciate it."

"Of course. I want answers also."

She shook her head and stared out the window. "This seems like a nightmare I should wake up from. Then I realize it's really happening. My friend is really missing."

Bear had the urge to reach over and squeeze her hand. But he didn't.

He liked Piper. But she was in the middle of serious emotional turmoil right now. It seemed wrong to concentrate on anything other than helping her—even if he *had* enjoyed the brief moment she'd been in his arms.

"I want to narrow down the suspect list," she continued. "I want to know for sure that those men ruled out earlier can be ruled out still. Maybe that's where I should have started."

"I'll do what I can to help."

Piper flashed a grateful smile. "Thank you."

Just then, his phone buzzed. Bear glanced at the screen and saw he'd received an alert. He'd set up several deep-level search terms, including those using the words rescue, mountains, Good Samaritan, and accident. Whenever a video was posted using those keywords, a notification was sent to him.

He clicked on the link and saw a new video had been posted.

Was it a video of Julie right before she died?

Bear's heart thrummed in his ears as he prayed that wasn't the case.

CHAPTER
SIXTEEN

PIPER SAW Bear's eyes widen, and she knew something was wrong.

"What is it?" she rushed.

He glanced up at her, something close to an apology in his gaze. "It's a new video."

The breath left her lungs. "Of Julie?"

Piper almost didn't want to know the answer to that question.

"I don't know. I haven't clicked on it yet."

She leaned closer, her heart pounding in her ears. "I need to know."

Bear glanced at her, studying her gaze. "Are you sure?"

Piper nodded. "I'm positive."

He studied her another moment before nodding and pressing Play.

She could hardly breathe as she watched the screen.

A woman in the frames—too far away to make out details—darted across an icy lake.

Fog Lake?

Based on the angle of the video, Piper couldn't be sure.

She held her breath as she continued watching.

All of a sudden, she disappeared.

The ice broke, Piper realized.

The woman had fallen in the water.

Piper's heart pounded harder.

A man's arms could be seen as he ran toward her. The images were shaky with his movement.

"Did you see that?" The man's voice sounded raspy as he dragged in shallow breaths. "That woman just fell through the ice. If she's not rescued soon, she'll go into hypothermia. I've got to see what I can do."

He continued to rush across the ice. His steps slowed as he approached the crack.

Even on the video, it was clear to see the breaks in the icy surface.

One wrong move, and that man could find himself in trouble also.

The next instant, the camera jostled, and the man dropped to his stomach. He must have moved the camera and strapped it to his forehead. It was the only thing that made sense.

He plunged his hand in the water, grunting and muttering prayers.

After several tries, he pulled his hand out.

He gripped something . . . the woman's arm.

Was it Julie?

Piper could hardly watch. Yet she couldn't look away either.

"I've got you," the man muttered. "I've got you."

He continued to struggle until the woman emerged from the lake and sprawled on the ice. Her sopping wet, dark hair nearly froze in the frigid air, and her lips looked blue even on the grainy video.

Piper's gaze remained riveted to the screen as she waited to see the woman's face.

But mostly all she saw was the deathly pale skin. The frosty hair.

Finally, she got a glimpse.

She released her breath.

That wasn't Julie.

She didn't recognize the woman—but Piper still prayed for her.

But, thank goodness, it wasn't her friend.

This video only proved her hypothesis.

The GSK hadn't acted alone.

His understudy had been awakened.

And, unless they stopped him, this video was probably only the first of many more to come.

———————

Bear headed back to the sheriff's office to report the video. It seemed easier to explain in person. But as he and Piper walked toward the door, reporters surrounded them.

"Aren't you Bear Colson?"

"How does your father feel about this new development?"

"Was your father working with someone from prison? Do you know the woman who's missing?"

Bear kept an arm around Piper and ushered her inside, away from the swarm of vipers.

Shane steered them toward the conference room, casting a final glance at the reporters outside the door.

"Sorry about that," he muttered. "They're vultures out there. This has quickly become a national news story, and every network is trying to get a leg up on the other."

"It's okay." Bear tried to shrug it off. "Reporters are the least of my concern at the moment."

Before they reached the conference room, two sheriff's deputies pushed through the back door, a handcuffed man between them. "I didn't do anything! You have no right to bring me here. I'm innocent!"

Bear recognized the man as Anthony Newton—Ralph's son.

Did they think he was the Understudy?

His heart beat harder.

Before anything else happened, the deputies steered Anthony into an interrogation room.

Was Anthony guilty? Or was he being tarred and feathered—just like Bear's father had been?

Shane ushered them into the conference room and crossed his arms as he turned toward them, not bothering to sit.

"What's going on?" Shane asked.

Bear showed him the video footage.

Shane's expression darkened as he watched. "I'm going to need for you to send me a link to that."

"I'll do that now."

"So, if this guy has a new victim, what did he do with Julie?" As Shane asked the question, he motioned for other agents to come into the room to see the video.

"Maybe Julie is still alive. Otherwise, she'd be the one in the video, right?" Piper stared back and forth between Bear and Shane with hopeful eyes.

"There's a good chance that's true," Shane

muttered. "But, if that's the case, where is this guy keeping her?"

That was a good question.

Shane muttered something to the other agents who'd flooded the room, and Bear knew their time here was quickly coming to an end. As it should.

These guys needed to investigate what had happened to the woman in this video. They needed to find her, and the lake at the center of town was large. It would take time to search the area—if it was even filmed at Fog Lake to begin with.

They couldn't let this guy kill anyone else.

There had already been too many lives lost.

CHAPTER
SEVENTEEN

DARKNESS WAS BEGINNING to settle around them as Piper and Bear headed back to his place. Normally, it would be dinnertime. But Piper had no desire to eat.

It had been a long day—and not much progress had been made.

It was frustrating, but that was the nature of investigations. Piper had learned that through her years of police work. But when a case was personal, everything felt more complicated.

"What are you thinking about?" Bear asked.

Piper shrugged as she thought about Bear's question. "My thoughts are bouncing all over the place right now. I hardly even know what to think."

"I can imagine."

"When we get back to your place, I'd like to look

over our suspects again. I want to really dig in and rule some people out. Like Anthony, for example. Why did the FBI bring him in for questioning?"

"That's a good question. Could it have something to do with the paranoia everyone around town has been experiencing?"

"Possibly."

Bear cast a glance at her. "What if the killer isn't someone on your list?"

Piper frowned. Bear had a valid question. Maybe they were totally off-base. Maybe the person behind these crimes was completely off their radar.

The thought wasn't comforting.

"I don't know," Piper said. "I don't want to waste time—that's not an option right now. I have to find Julie before it's too late."

"I know the FBI is working nonstop on locating her."

"But what if that's not enough?" Her voice cracked, and she glanced out the window before Bear could see how upset she was.

Bear grabbed her hand, his strong fingers closing over hers. "Just try to stay positive."

Piper sniffled as she held back tears. "I'm trying to. But it's so hard."

"I'll go through that list with you when we get

back to my place. We'll divide out the names and see if we can check alibis. We'll get through this."

She sniffed again, trying to hold back her emotions. The fact that Bear was willing to help her meant the world to her. Ever since Piper had been fired, she'd felt so alone. Her professional contacts had also been her friends, and she felt like she'd lost both in one fell swoop.

She hadn't really acknowledged that fact until this moment.

Even with Julie and Luna, it wasn't the same.

"Thanks for your support," she told Bear. "I can't tell you how much it means to me."

"Of course. Whatever you need, just let me know."

Could Piper really depend on Bear? She wanted to believe she could. But she'd been fooled before, and she didn't want to take the chance of being played again. But Bear seemed so sincere . . . why shouldn't she trust him?

Maybe it was because the worst kind of hurt didn't come from enemies—it came from those you trusted.

Like Tim.

Tim had not only been her colleague. Through working together, they'd grown close. They'd begun seeing each other in secret. Much like Piper and Bear, working on cases together had bonded them.

But it had all been a mistake to trust Tim.

Piper had vowed never to make such errors again.

Was that what Bear would become? A mistake?

She wanted to believe he wouldn't.

But she no longer trusted her instincts.

In her line of work, that was a problem that could end up costing lives.

———

Bear and Piper had worked side-by-side in companionable silence for an hour before Bear looked up from his computer. He'd brought it to the kitchen table so he and Piper could talk through any findings. They were both going down their list of suspects independently before comparing notes.

He'd set out a few snacks to munch on in place of dinner—some cashews, crackers, and grapes, along with cheese for Piper.

"Okay, this is what I've got so far," he started.

Piper pulled her chair over to see his hand-scribbled notes.

"We can rule out Kevin Black," Bear started.

"He's been out of town for the past ten days on a vacation with his new girlfriend."

"Noted." Piper crossed his name off her list.

"Skip Johnson is wearing an ankle monitor while he's on parole. The FBI would have picked up on his involvement by now."

"True." She crossed another name off.

"Leonard Kincy is on dialysis," Bear continued. "I have a hard time believing someone in his weakened state would be able to grab a twenty-six-year-old woman in a mine or even pull someone out of an icy lake, for that matter."

"I agree." Another name marked off.

"Rod Wilkins was at a fundraiser event for children in foster care," Bear continued. "There are pictures of him all over social media. The event took place at the same time Julie was abducted."

Piper sighed. "Our list is getting shorter."

Bear let out a long breath. "I made a few phone calls and discovered that Arnie Siebert was emceeing a birthday party up at Shady Oaks Campground today. That's why we saw him coming down the road when we were at Falling Timbers."

Piper nodded slowly. "Doesn't necessarily mean he's innocent."

"True. I also heard that Arnie has taken a job with

Buildings and Inspection for the town. Maybe being an emcee isn't as profitable as he'd hoped."

"Do you know if he was working on Monday when Julie was taken?"

"I actually asked about that. It turns out he was out doing some inspections. Doesn't have an alibi."

"Good to know."

"I also can't find an alibi for Ted Russo or Harry Simpkins at the time of Julie's abduction. However, I also haven't talked to them personally."

"You searched their social media?"

"I did." Bear offered a quick nod. "Arnie is the only one who actively engages in social media, however."

Piper leaned back and let out a sigh. "Harry would have been teaching at the time Julie was snatched. It should be easy to find out whether or not he was at work."

"I'll ask someone I know who works at the school with him."

"Perfect." Piper grabbed the notebook in front of her. "What about Anthony, the man we saw being brought in today?"

"He was working at the hospital all day."

"I wonder why they brought him in then . . ." Piper nibbled on her bottom lip.

"Good question."

REFUGE OF REDEMPTION 139

She let out a breath. "Now I can share what I discovered."

Bear turned in his chair toward her, interested in what she'd learned. "Whenever you're ready."

Her gaze lit with a moment of excitement as she started. "It turns out that Arnie and Ralph Burgess were good friends."

Bear's eyes widened. "How did you figure that out?"

"I did an image search online, and I found photos of them together at several events. They posed together as if they were best friends."

"That is interesting."

"Something else interesting . . . Ted Russo's dad used to work at the mine."

Bear's eyebrows climbed again. "It looks like we might have two decent suspects."

Piper nodded as she stared at her list. "It does. But figuring out more information could be tricky."

However, neither Piper nor Bear would let that stop them.

CHAPTER
EIGHTEEN

JUST AS BEAR and Piper wrapped up their conversation on suspects, Piper's phone buzzed. It was Luna.

Luna?

Piper was surprised her intern was calling after yesterday's blowup.

She swallowed hard before putting the phone to her ear. "Hey, Luna."

"Hey, Piper." Luna sounded hushed. "Any updates?"

Piper glanced at the list in front of her. "Not yet. But we're doing everything we can to find Julie."

"I still can't believe she's gone." Luna's voice cracked.

"Neither can I." Piper paused, her thoughts racing. "Do your parents know you're calling?"

"No, I didn't tell them."

A knot formed in her throat. "Luna . . . I don't want you to get into more trouble."

"I know. But they're overreacting . . ."

Piper agreed but . . . "They're still your parents, and you have to respect their wishes."

"You're probably right, but I don't have time to talk about this right now. There's something I need to tell you."

Piper froze at the ominous sound of her voice. She glanced at Bear, who'd leaned closer to listen.

"I'm going to put you on speaker so Professor Colson can hear. Is that okay?"

"Sure," Luna rushed. "Julie lost her wallet a couple weeks ago, which isn't like her. She's usually so organized. Anyway, afterward, I got her one of those tracking tiles."

Piper paused, not wanting to jump to conclusions —but another part of her wanted to dive right in and immerse herself in the pool of possibilities. "Was her wallet in her backpack?"

"It was."

Piper's heart beat harder. "Do you know what kind of tracking tile it was or if there's a way we can locate it?"

"Actually, when Julie and I were trying to figure out how to use it, I downloaded the app on my phone so I could show her it was safe—she has that thing about not downloading strange apps. Anyway, I never deleted the app, and I have a location marked for her tracking tile."

"What?" The air left Piper's lungs. "Can you send it to me?"

"I will." She lowered her voice. "I'll do it as soon as I'm off the phone. Listen, I hear my parents, so I need to go. Keep me updated if you can!"

Before Piper could say anything else, the call ended.

A tracking tile . . .

Piper turned to Bear and saw the excitement in his gaze also.

This could be the lead they'd been looking for.

———

Bear couldn't believe his ears.

Not only did Julie have a tracking tile in her backpack, but Luna had the app loaded on her phone?

This could be just what they needed to find Julie.

"Did Luna send it yet?" He scooted closer to Piper and glanced at her phone.

Piper stared at her screen. "I'm expecting it at any minute. Come on, Luna . . . we don't have time to waste."

As soon as Piper had a location, she would let the FBI know. She couldn't put the investigation at risk by doing anything foolhardy. After supposedly ruining that last case, she knew she had to tread carefully.

Finally, Luna's email came through.

Bear slid his chair closer and peered over her shoulder.

With a trembling hand, Piper clicked on the tracking link and waited for the page to populate. Finally, a map appeared.

"Zoom in," Bear directed.

Piper enlarged the map as she scrambled to make sense of what she was seeing. She didn't know the Fog Lake area well enough to know exactly what area she was looking at.

"It looks like the middle of nowhere," Piper muttered.

Bear flinched before leaning back and raking a hand through his hair.

"What is it?" Piper rushed.

"That location . . . it's here on my property."

"What?" Piper's voice sounded breathless.

Bear rushed to his feet. "Come on. We have to check this out. Now."

CHAPTER
NINETEEN

PIPER COULD HARDLY KEEP up with Bear as he pulled his coat on and rushed into the dark outdoors. He'd grabbed a flashlight, and it flickered on, the beam lighting a path in front of them.

Was Julie really being kept here on Bear's property?

What sense would that make?

Unless someone wanted to plant suspicion on Bear.

Based on his reaction, he was just as surprised as Piper at the location where the pin had been dropped.

Piper knew Bear wasn't guilty. Someone was just trying to play games.

That's what this guy did.

Bear kept the map app open on his phone as he

rushed into the woods. Piper had sent him the location since he knew this property better than she did. She followed behind him as he wove between the barren winter trees and dodged tripping hazards on the rocky surface.

As he paused, Piper stopped, her heart pounding out of control.

She pulled her coat closer around her neck as her blood turned as ice cold as the stream.

Bear raised his phone and glanced around. "According to this, we're practically on top of the tracker."

Piper didn't think of herself as someone easily spooked. But right now, she couldn't shake the tremble consuming her.

Bear took a few more steps and swept his flashlight over the ground. "It says we're here."

Piper glanced around, observing that there was nothing of note in this area. No rock formations. No natural overhangs. No old outbuildings.

"It doesn't make any sense," Bear muttered.

Piper's gaze stopped on a pile of leaves gathered against a cluster of trees. Out of curiosity, she used her foot to shuffle part of the pile aside.

She held her breath as fabric peeked through.

Her heart pounded harder.

Was Julie buried beneath these leaves?

Bear saw the fear on Piper's face and pushed her behind him. "Let me."

Using his foot, Bear swept away a few more leaves and shone the beam of his flashlight on the ground.

A backpack came into view.

Was there a body with it?

Swallowing hard, he brushed away several more leaves.

Bear released his breath at what he saw.

No body.

Just a backpack.

"Julie's not here," he told Piper quietly.

Her shoulders visibly sank with relief when she heard the news. "Thank God."

"But that still doesn't explain why her backpack is here." He pulled out his phone. "I need to let Shane know."

More than anything, he wanted to dive into the contents of the bag, to see if any clues had been left inside.

But he knew better than to disturb any potential evidence that may have been left.

As they waited for the FBI to show up, Bear noted that Piper's skin looked pale and her eyes full of fear.

"It's okay," he murmured.

Bear reached for her and, the next instant, she was in his arms. He held her tight, pulling her head against his chest.

He wished he could take away her pain, that he could magically make things right.

If only it were possible in a situation like this.

Before Bear could relish how perfectly Piper fit into his arms, something on a nearby tree caught his eye. A red light.

His breath caught.

Was that . . .

It was.

A trail camera. The red light indicated it was recording.

Which meant someone was watching their every move right now. That same person was probably enjoying Piper's grief a little too much.

He turned away from the camera, determined not to entertain someone at Piper's expense. His determination to find a killer was quickly turning into anger.

This man was playing games, and Bear didn't like it.

CHAPTER
TWENTY

"BEAR?" Piper glanced at Bear as she noticed him stiffen. "What is it?"

"I didn't put that trail camera there."

Slowly, she turned her head until her gaze stopped at the device perched on a beech tree. "Does it look like the ones you saw on the way to the mine?"

"As a matter of fact, yes, it does. Someone has made himself comfortable on my property." Bear practically growled as he said the words.

Piper's spine stiffened. "What do we do?"

"I'm staying with this evidence until the FBI gets here. But I'm not going to give this guy a show either." He turned again, his back to the camera.

Piper followed suit. "Isn't there a way to trace where that footage is being sent?"

"Not that I know of. But you better believe I'm going to see what I can figure out."

Piper's thoughts raced. How could this monster always be a few steps ahead of them? It made no sense.

"This guy is sick," she finally muttered. "He gets his thrills off other people's grief and suffering. There should be a special kind of punishment for people like him."

"I agree. This guy likes playing with our heads."

"I know. We tried to narrow this down to our top two suspects—Arnie and Ted. But I have to admit that between both of them . . . neither strike me as tech savvy."

"True. I think the person responsible for these crimes knows exactly what he's doing," Bear said. "He knows how cameras work. How social media works. How to put together a video."

"He was also smart enough to leave clues in those videos and photos," Piper added. "I'm liking this less and less all the time. It's one thing to go up against a criminal who doesn't know what they're doing."

"But someone this meticulous . . ." Bear shook his head.

A knot formed in her throat. "Exactly. But we're going to keep digging, and we're going to find some answers." She stared at her friend's dark green back-

REFUGE OF REDEMPTION   151

pack, still partially buried by dry leaves. "Do you think the killer left a clue inside?"

"I wouldn't put it past him. He wants to toy with us. He wants to let us know he's smarter than we are."

"It was almost like he knew we were going to find that tracking tile. That's why he left it here." Piper crossed her arms.

Bear frowned and rubbed his jaw. "You're right. He must have gone through her things, found it, and planted it here knowing we'd eventually figure out she had that tile."

Piper glanced around at the secluded area. There weren't any close access points that she could tell. "How is it possible that someone came back this way without you seeing? Isn't there only one road leading to your property?"

"There are a couple of small service roads used mostly by the county that run alongside my property on this side of the mountain. It would be probably a mile or two to hike in from one of them. But it is possible someone could've used one of those."

Piper let out a long breath as her thoughts churned. "The other night when I was looking outside . . . and I felt certain that somebody was watching us. It looks like I wasn't wrong."

"I think this guy is terrified you might have

answers. That's one more reason why he wants to play games with you now."

Piper couldn't argue with Bear's assessment.

She could feel the danger around her growing stronger and stronger by the moment.

———

Shane and two other agents arrived thirty minutes later.

"We need to check the area around here, just to make sure there are no other clues," Shane said, his words brisk. "We'll take it from here."

Bear felt reluctant to leave the evidence they'd found. But he knew there was no arguing with the FBI. Besides, that was why Bear had called them. They needed to do their job.

He knew the feds were busy right now trying to find the woman from the video. That was one of their first priorities. But maybe this backpack would provide clues.

Piper stepped closer to Shane, something close to desperation in her gaze. "If there's anything of interest inside the backpack, will you let me know?"

Shane turned toward her. "Do you have any idea what Ms. Anderson would have put inside? It's going to be hard to know if there's anything unusual, since we didn't know what was in it in the first place."

Piper stared at the backpack, an almost glazed look in her eyes. "I was with Julie when she packed it. I could probably give you a good idea if there's anything out of the ordinary."

"In a few minutes, when we're done here, I'll bring the backpack to your place, Bear, and see what we find." Shane glanced at him, waiting for his approval.

Bear nodded. "Of course. Also, I might be able to find out where the images are being sent on that trail cam. If you're willing to let me help, I'll do what I can."

"I just might take you up on that offer," Shane said. "For now, you two go home and warm up. We'll be there in a little while."

Bear and Piper were quiet as they headed back to Bear's place.

Bear could see the exhaustion—and preoccupation—in Piper's eyes. She'd been through a lot, and the end wasn't in sight yet.

Twenty minutes later, he ushered her into his house, hoping the change of scenery would do her good.

But as soon as he took his coat off at the front door, he froze.

Something felt different.

"What is it?" Piper asked as she scanned the space around them.

Bear remained near the door, looking around and trying to figure out the source of his unease.

He sucked in a quick breath when he spotted what he was looking for.

A device was perched in a corner above his kitchen cabinet.

A small camera.

While he and Piper had been out investigating the backpack, the killer had been in Bear's house.

That monster had planted this camera so he could watch and listen to their every move.

Anger churned in his gut.

Just what else had this guy done? What else had he left?

"Bear?" Piper's voice rose with anxiety.

"Someone's been in the house . . ." he muttered. "Stay here."

He needed to search his house and make sure this guy wasn't still here. He didn't think he was, but he had to be certain.

After he made sure this monster was gone, he'd search every inch of this place until he found what else this guy might have done.

CHAPTER
TWENTY-ONE

PIPER WATCHED as the FBI swept Bear's house.

She stood against the wall near the front door, trying to stay out of their way.

But she couldn't shake the eerie feeling consuming her.

The person behind this . . . he was determined. Smart. Sick.

Piper had convinced herself that she was strong enough to defeat the monster perpetrating these crimes. But what if she wasn't?

She swallowed hard and pressed herself into the wall.

"I checked the footage from my security cameras," Bear announced as he walked down the stairs, his presence easily filling the room. "Whoever came here must have known about my cameras. The power to them has been cut."

"Did you get any images of this person before the power died?" Townsend abandoned his examination of the living room and stepped closer to Bear.

Bear scowled. "No, I didn't. This guy must have come around the side of the house so the cameras wouldn't catch sight of him. He was able to pinpoint the blind spot."

"He's smart," Townsend muttered, his hands going to his hips.

"Maybe a little too smart." Bear's eyebrows pushed together.

Townsend let out a long breath and glanced around. "My guys have swept the rest of the house. They found two more cameras and several listening devices. As you know, the footage is probably being sent to a website that's being opened on the dark web. By the time we track down one location, he'll simply have changed it to another."

Bear scowled again. "It just seems like there should be *something* we can do."

"We'll keep working on it. I'm guessing that this guy sees you as a threat. That's why he wanted to monitor you, to see how close to the truth you're getting."

"Is Anthony a suspect?" Bear got right to the point.

Townsend's gaze darkened. "He was exploring the North Elk Ridge Mine. Someone else saw him go inside, and one of my agents caught him. When we questioned him, he said his father asked him to see what was inside. We charged him with trespassing, but he's out on bail."

"So, you don't think he has anything to do with this?" Piper asked.

"As of right now, no."

"What about the backpack?" Piper asked, wanting to make sure it hadn't been forgotten—nor had Julie.

Townsend sent her a quick nod. "I was just getting to that. How about if we go through that now? You can tell me if anything seems unusual inside."

She nodded, feeling halfway numb as she wondered what they'd find. She wanted to help. But she also feared she might stumble across something horrific, something that would forever stain her mind.

Trepidation filled her as she walked toward the kitchen counter. Bear seemed to sense her distress and remained close. She appreciated his attentiveness.

She'd feared when she met him the first time that he wouldn't be anything like the person she'd conjured in her mind. And he wasn't.

He was even better.

It was too bad Piper had sworn off dating.

They paused at the counter, and Townsend pulled on some gloves. Carefully, he opened the backpack and began pulling out various contents.

A water bottle. Some dried fruit and beef jerky. An extra set of gloves, sunscreen, Chapstick.

Julie had always liked to be prepared.

So far, nothing was out of the ordinary.

He grabbed Julie's wallet and riffled through it a moment.

The tracking tile slid onto the table.

Just like Luna had said.

At the very bottom of the backpack, there was a photo.

Piper sucked in a breath.

It was of Piper and Bear walking through downtown Fog Lake.

This guy was taunting them. He wanted to let them know that he was hidden in plain sight. And he was tracking their every move.

———

After the FBI left, Bear called his friend who worked at the high school. She verified that Simpkins had been at school all week. If that was true, then Simpkins couldn't have abducted Julie. They could rule him out.

His and Piper's best bet was to figure out where the trail cam footage was being sent.

"You think you can figure out who the killer is based on the trail cams?" Piper asked as they sat on the couch beside each other.

Bear stared at his computer screen, wishing he could press a few keys and find answers. "It's like Shane and I talked about—this guy is smart. He's probably running everything through the dark web. It's unlikely I'll be able to find anything out because of the layered encryption. But I'm going to try."

Piper tucked her legs under her and leaned toward him.

Bear was all too aware of her presence—entirely more than he wanted to be.

He didn't easily trust people, and every time he had, he'd regretted it. His dad had chosen to go to jail rather than to reveal who his secret girlfriend was. His aunt had threatened to frame him as the GSK if he didn't walk away from his brother and sister. His brother and sister had been estranged from him for more than a decade because of trust issues. Then he'd finally given someone a chance—Sasha—and she'd used him.

His track record was abysmal.

However, there was something about Piper that made him want to try again.

Still, deep inside, he knew that was a bad idea.

He typed something into the computer. "This is going to take a while . . ." he muttered.

"I understand." Piper yawned. "I don't have anything to do but wait."

Several minutes later, her head hit his shoulder. Bear started to say something to her when he glanced over.

She'd fallen asleep.

A smile tugged at his lips.

He considered waking her but decided not to.

He'd let her rest for a while . . . and he'd enjoy the moment while it lasted.

CHAPTER
TWENTY-TWO

NOTHING BROUGHT me more delight than seeing the shock on Bear Colson's face when he found that camera in his house.

I knew he'd find it.

I waited until I saw him and Piper leave.

Then I moved in.

It was too easy, really. I'd expected more of a challenge. But the security cameras were easy to take out. The other equipment I'd left had been simple to install.

And it was all worth it.

I glance at the woman I've abducted.

Julie has been quiet. Resilient. No matter what I do, she won't talk. Won't tell me what Piper knows.

So, I've had to resort to other means necessary to get her to share information with me.

Bringing Julie to this location was risky. Very risky. But I've ensured that she won't get away. Even if she were to escape, she'd have nowhere to go.

I smile.

I love being smarter than everyone else.

I don't know when my next kill will be.

I know I should probably wait awhile.

But toying with investigators is so much fun.

Decisions, decisions . . .

I tap my fingers against my thigh as I think.

I know what I *want* to do, but I've found it prudent to resist my impulses.

It's how I've eluded capture for so long.

I'll continue to evade authorities.

You'll see.

But just sitting here and doing nothing won't satisfy me.

I need people to know I have power over them—power to cause fear and terror.

I'm one man, and I've changed the actions of hundreds of people, people who now lock their doors at night, who won't go anywhere alone after dark.

That's clout.

I'll show the people of Fog Lake they need to continue living in fear of me.

I step away from the woman so I can get ready for work.

It's going to be a beautiful day.

A beautiful day to cause despair.

CHAPTER
TWENTY-THREE

PIPER HAD WOKEN up to find herself on the couch with a blanket tucked around her.

Her cheeks heated at the thought of it.

How had she ended up there?

The last thing she remembered was talking to Bear, sitting next to him. Then she'd woken up this morning.

Had she fallen asleep on his shoulder?

She didn't know. But she hadn't had the nerve to ask Bear during breakfast. Instead, she'd pretended like nothing happened.

She'd offered to clean up afterward since Bear had to teach his Architecture of a Secure Operating System class.

In a way, she was glad Bear had to teach. She could use some space to gather her thoughts.

After she cleaned the kitchen, she sat on the couch with her laptop and studied the crime-scene photos again. If that map leading to the mine had been deliberately planted, then there had to be other things also in these photos. There had to be something she hadn't picked up on before. It only made sense.

As she sipped her coffee—brewed by Bear before he began teaching his class—she pulled up the first image and studied it. Even though she'd already done it once, she made a list of every item in every photo. Nothing was too small.

The problem was, so many years had passed that it was nearly impossible to know what belonged and what didn't.

What was Piper missing?

As she worked, her phone buzzed. She glanced at the screen and saw Phil, her former boss with the Chicago PD, was calling.

Why was he trying to get in touch?

The man was abrasive, to say the least. He was head of forensics, and he was unyielding. He hadn't been her favorite person—especially not after he'd fired her.

With both curiosity and trepidation coursing through her, she hit Talk. "Hey, Phil."

"Piper. I saw you on the news." His words came out fast and clipped.

"I was on the news?" Had she missed something?

"Yeah, yeah. You were shown going into the sheriff's office in Fog Lake. You helping with the GSK case?"

She remembered all the vulture-like reporters who'd been outside of the sheriff's office with their microphones and cameras and frowned. "Not officially."

"Look, Piper . . . I've gotta say that I think you're a top-notch forensic photographer and one of the best image analysts I've ever met."

Piper narrowed her eyes. "That's not what you said when you fired me." In fact, compliments from him were very rare and had come only when he'd wanted something.

"I know, I know. However, you put me in a tough position."

She lowered her voice as bad memories flooded back to her. "You know I would have never done something like that."

"I want to believe that. Look, that's why I called. I wanted to let you know that, if you restore your reputation, I'll think about rehiring you."

Piper sat up straighter, unsure if she'd heard correctly. "What?"

"I mean it. If you're able to help with this high-profile case, then I'll consider giving you another chance."

"You mean it? I thought . . ." She never thought anyone would ever hire her again. Working for herself had sounded glamorous, but it had been a real strain on her budget. Trying to find contract work after what had happened . . . it was hard.

She didn't tell many people, but she'd even taken a few gigs as a wedding and newborn photographer to help pay her bills.

"Yeah, really."

Piper nibbled on her bottom lip. On one hand, his offer seemed too good to be true. On the other hand, was Phil just using her as a public relations stunt? And, even if that was true, would it be worth being used if it meant getting her old job back and salvaging her career?

She licked her lips as the questions collided in her head.

"I'll keep you updated," she finally told him.

"Good. You do that. This could be your chance to make things right."

Piper felt the pressure mounting in her chest.

Make things right?

She hadn't been the one to make things wrong to begin with. Tim had. And he'd gotten away with it.

The last thing she wanted to do was to put herself in a vulnerable position . . . again.

————

Bear came downstairs in time to hear the end of Piper's phone conversation.

What was that about?

He waved to let her know he was there, not wanting to eavesdrop. She flashed a quick, almost uneasy smile before ending her conversation and turning toward him.

"Everything okay?" He slowly lowered himself into the chair beside her, hoping he wasn't interrupting something.

"Just one of my old colleagues," she quickly explained.

"I see."

She pushed a hair behind her ear, clearly not wanting to talk about it anymore. "How was your class?"

"Uneventful. My next one isn't for five more hours, so I have a break."

"Why do you teach?" Piper studied his face with open curiosity. "Why not work in the field?"

Bear let out a long breath as he contemplated his answer. "Honestly? I have a basic distrust for police, I guess, especially after everything that happened with my father. I wanted to influence a generation of up-and-coming investigators. I thought I could do the most good there."

"I understand." She offered another soft smile. "I've always wondered that. I hope you don't mind me asking."

"It's no problem."

"By the way, I just happened to walk by your office while you were teaching, and I caught a glimpse of some students in your class."

"Okay . . ." He had no idea where she was going with this.

"Do you think it's strange that most of your students are women?"

Bear shrugged. "Not really. Why?"

Piper shrugged, though the twinkle in her eyes made it clear there was more to it. "Just an observation. Statistically speaking, most people who work in the tech field are men. It just seems weird that your students skew to mostly female . . . and that they all look at you with stars in their eyes."

Bear let out a chuckle as he realized what she was getting at. "I assure you, my students are there to learn."

"And to stare at their handsome professor." She

let out a dramatic sigh and clasped her hands over her heart.

He shook his head. "I doubt that. I'm sure they all have the most upright of intentions."

Piper let out a teasing grunt. "I'm sure."

He shifted in his seat as he thought about his real reason for finding Piper. He wanted nothing more than to keep their lighthearted conversation going. But that wasn't an option right now.

"By the way, I came down to let you know that Shane is on his way over," Bear started. "He has an update to share."

Piper's gaze dimmed as questions raced through her eyes.

Curiosity. Realization. Fear.

"Is it about Julie? Do you think they found her?"

Compassion panged inside him. "He didn't say. I'm sorry."

Piper let out a breath as she tucked her legs beneath her, suddenly more somber. "It just doesn't make sense why this guy would hold Julie this long. I'm grateful there aren't any signs he's killed her, of course. But I'm just trying to figure out what his next move might be. I'm trying to get into his head."

"A nearly impossible task."

She frowned and took another sip of her coffee. "I know. I never expected any of this when I came here.

I thought Julie, Luna, and I would head back home to Lexington that night after we found the mine entrance. That we'd return to life as normal. Not anything like this."

"Life certainly does take unexpected turns sometimes."

They exchanged a knowing look.

"Yes, it does," Piper finally said.

"Speaking of Julie and Luna . . . how did the three of you meet?" Bear needed to do something to keep her thoughts occupied until Shane got here.

Piper shifted and let out a long breath. "Julie read about my work and reached out, saying she'd love to learn from me and that she didn't believe any of the rumors about me. She'd studied criminology but decided she didn't want to be a police officer. She wants to go into forensics instead. She has all the right chops for it."

"And Luna?"

"Luna is a sophomore at the University of Kentucky. She called me one day a couple of months ago and asked if she could intern under me. She said when she heard I lived in Lexington, it seemed like a no-brainer. She follows crime stories and thought it would be a good opportunity. I told her I couldn't pay her. I can barely pay Julie. Who am I kidding? I can barely pay myself."

"If you don't mind me asking . . . how do you pay yourself?" Bear asked. "I mean, what exactly are you doing?"

"I've been doing some photoshop work for some magazines, as well as portrait photography, to pay my bills. I've been hoping that a police department will ask for my help, but so far I haven't had any bites. I'm not really surprised . . ."

"Maybe with some time."

She let out a sigh. "I review past cases with Julie and Luna so I can teach them how forensic photography works. It's . . . fulfilling, actually. But I don't know how long I can keep this up. I'm going to have to make some decisions soon about my future and if I should stay in this field or not."

"Does Luna want to go into forensics also?"

"Either that or criminology. She's still trying to narrow it down—and her sophomore year is a great time to do that. She has an amazing memory. Ask her about any serial killer in the United States, and she'll be able to quote anything you need to know about them."

"It seems like the three of you are quite the trio."

"We are. Julie has more experience, so I talk things through with her a lot. Luna is starting at the bottom, so to speak. I have her do research and fetch coffee and file papers. I haven't shown her all the crime-scene photos I'm examining yet. I'm not sure she's ready for that, even though I know she wants to be ready. She wants to be right in the mix with me and Julie, but I think she needs more time."

Before they could talk more, tires crunched across the gravel driveway.

Shane must be here.

Bear couldn't wait to hear what Shane had to say. But he prayed, for Piper's sake, that it wasn't bad news.

CHAPTER
TWENTY-FOUR

PIPER COULD HARDLY SIT STILL as she waited to hear Townsend's update.

He sat with them at the kitchen table, coffee in front of him, before speaking. "We've IDed the woman from the video—the one who 'fell' into the icy lake."

Piper held her breath as she waited for more information.

"Her name is Jen Allendale," Townsend continued. "She's a local. Twenty-five years old."

"That name sounds familiar," Bear muttered.

"Jen's dad works for Fog Lake Public Utilities. Her mom taught piano lessons to about half the kids in town."

"Did you find Jen . . . in the lake?" Piper hardly

wanted to ask the question. But she couldn't get those images out of her head.

Townsend's lips flickered down in a frown. "We did. It was a risky operation, considering the condition of the ice. Plus, the hole she fell through had iced over again, but our guys managed to find her and pull her out. Her parents frantically called everyone yesterday when she didn't come home from work."

"I'm so sorry to hear that," Piper muttered. "I can't imagine what they must be going through."

"Were initials carved into her arm?" Bear asked.

Townsend nodded somberly. "They were, and a cross necklace hung around her neck. This was his work."

A chill washed through Piper. "Do you think he left any other clues at the crime scene? Or in the videos?"

"Funny you brought that up." Townsend shifted. "Since you mentioned that this guy had done that before, I took a good look at the video, trying to see if anything was out of place. Our victim was actually wearing earrings that didn't belong to her."

"Is that right?" Piper sounded breathless as she asked the question.

He pulled out his phone and showed her a picture. "These are what they looked like."

Piper glanced at the photograph and sucked in a

breath when she saw the gold feather earrings. "Those are . . . mine."

Townsend's eyebrows flickered up. "What?"

"I left them on the nightstand upstairs. Someone must have . . ." She couldn't bring herself to finish the statement.

"I'll get someone over to dust for prints."

"You won't find any," Bear said. "This guy is too smart for that."

Piper sucked in a deep breath, trying to keep her emotions in check. "What about the other bodies from the tunnel. Did you ID any more of them?"

"We did. They're all women. Some were from this area, but most of the victims were from surrounding towns. Most of them had little to no family and friends, so no one noticed when they went missing."

"That's a shame." Bear's jaw seemed to tighten, and he ran a hand over it.

"More and more reporters are showing up," Townsend continued. "Even the guy from *Dateline* arrived to do a show on what's been happening here. As far as the residents here, I've never seen this town as quiet as I did last night when I left the sheriff's office. Everyone seems to be staying inside and locking their doors."

"As they should . . ." Bear mumbled. "No one wants to take a chance."

"You're right. Everyone should be scared." Townsend nodded, the motion stiff and somber. "There's one other thing I thought you should know."

"What's that?" Bear asked.

Townsend hesitated a moment. "I probably shouldn't mention this to you. But . . . Jen Allendale . . . she worked for Parks and Recreation here in town."

"That's where Ted Russo works," Piper blurted.

Townsend nodded grimly. "Yes, it is. I'm not saying he's guilty. But we did bring him in for questioning. He refused to talk, and we didn't have enough evidence to hold him. But he is a person of interest."

———

Shane had just left when Isaac showed up. Bear ushered him inside, and he, Piper, and Isaac all stood in the kitchen sipping coffee as they talked about the latest updates. Word had quickly spread all over town about what had happened to Jen Allendale, even though no official statements from the FBI had been released.

"I vaguely remember Jen from growing up here." Isaac shook his head, the motion stiff with disbelief.

"She seemed nice. Rebecca knew her and thought highly of her. Everyone in town is so upset."

"I can imagine . . ." Piper muttered.

Isaac let out a sigh and lowered his coffee mug back onto the table before running a hand through his hair. "Anyway . . . that's not why I'm here. I have an update on Dad, and I thought you'd want to hear it in person."

Bear's spine stiffened. "What's going on?"

Even though someone else had been charged with the crimes James Colson was sent to prison for, the red tape to have him released had seemed insurmountable. It had been two weeks, and their father still hadn't been freed.

"If everything stays on track, he should be coming home by the end of this week," Isaac announced.

Bear's heart beat harder. "Really?"

Isaac cupped his coffee mug with his hands as he nodded. "Really. I can hardly believe it myself. It looks like it's really going to happen . . . finally."

Memories of Bear's last conversation with his dad flooded his mind. Their encounter hadn't been pleasant, and he wasn't sure their reunion would be as happy as everyone else might envision.

But Bear was glad justice would be served. His dad didn't deserve to be in prison for a crime he didn't commit. That was one thing his whole family could agree on.

"Thanks for letting me know." Bear took a sip of his coffee. "I take it you've already told Madison."

Isaac nodded. "She's thrilled. Talking about planning a coming home party and the whole works."

Bear wasn't sure he was ready to take it that far. But he was happy for his siblings. He'd only ever wanted what was best for them.

At times, Bear still felt a sting of bitterness when he thought about what they'd all been through. Anyone could look at his family and see that the hand life had given them wasn't fair. Those defining moments had ripple effects, still to this day.

Isaac glanced at the notebook beside him and squinted. "What's that? A list of Dad's favorite things?"

Piper pulled her notebook closer and glanced at her scribbled notes. "What? No. I'm listing things from crime scene photos, actually."

Tension tightened Bear's back muscles. "What do you mean 'Dad's favorite things'?"

Isaac blanched, and he waved a hand in the air. "It was nothing."

"Isaac, clearly, it was something." Bear stared at his brother, waiting to hear what he was thinking.

His brother shrugged. "It's just that I saw Big Red

chewing gum, a Cal Ripken Jr. baseball card, a pen from The Pancake Pantry in Gatlinburg. Those were all Dad's favorites. I thought . . ." Isaac shrugged again.

Bear felt everything go still around him.

That was a coincidence. That was all. It had to be.

But if that was true, then why did his head suddenly start spinning?

CHAPTER
TWENTY-FIVE

"I'M sure it's just a coincidence," Piper muttered, sensing the tension falling over Bear after Isaac's revelation.

"I wish I could believe that . . ." Bear ran a hand through his hair, leaving it in messy waves.

"Wait . . ." Isaac sat up straighter. "You think those items were planted on the victims?"

"We already know that map was planted," Bear said. "The original GSK probably didn't plant anything. But the Understudy probably did as a means of adding his own touch to the crimes."

"I can confirm that at least two victims died because of the man with a scarred hand in their videos." Piper almost didn't want to share that update. But Isaac and Bear deserved to know the truth. "I've looked at other people's hands as I've examined suspects. But I haven't seen anything that's raised red flags. The scar could have faded through the years."

"So, this guy wanted to set up Dad also . . ." Isaac muttered. "It wasn't a coincidence that Dad is in jail. The real killers wanted a scapegoat. Dad was targeted all along."

"Harry Simpkins makes the most sense then, right?" Piper asked. "He knew your father the best out of all the suspects. He would have known about the gum, the restaurant, the baseball card."

"That's a decent theory." Isaac shook his head, his gaze suddenly looking heavy. "I have no idea at this point. Was there anything else in those crime scene photos that offered any type of clue?"

"Not that I've put together yet." Piper's lips pulled down in a frown. "But I'm still looking."

"Keep doing that." Isaac's voice hardened. "We've got to end this. The last thing I want is for something like this to come out and somehow hinder Dad's chances of being released."

"You think the police could still believe Dad was somehow involved?" Bear stared at his brother as if shocked.

"Nothing would surprise me anymore." Isaac stared at Bear, something close to defeat in his gaze. "Nothing at all."

———

Isaac left a few minutes later, but Bear's mind was still reeling after their conversation.

He couldn't deny the proof in front of him. Someone had clearly wanted to target his dad. Had this monster been waiting for years for someone to discover that evidence pointing to his father?

He would hate for his family to have come this far only for some small clue to incriminate his father again. Bear couldn't let that happen.

On the other hand, this guy wanted it to be known that he was smart. That he'd left his own signatures in the videos of his kills.

Bear let out a sigh.

Was there anything else they were missing?

"I know this is a lot." Piper squeezed his hand. "I'm sorry. I had no idea those objects might point to your dad."

The feeling of Piper's hand covering his did amazing things to calm Bear's otherwise raging emotions. "I know you didn't. You were just following the evidence."

"I still feel like there's something else there in those photos, something I've missed." She shook her head as if frustrated with herself.

"I'll look at them with you, if you think that would help."

"Two heads are better than one, as the saying goes." Piper paused and glanced at her phone. She tapped an icon to open something.

"What is it?"

She pushed herself upright. "It's a video. Of Julie."

"What?" Bear's pitch heightened in surprise, and he leaned closer.

Piper's eyes remained fastened to the screen. Her friend's face stared into the camera, tears glistening in her eyes as darkness surrounded her.

Julie was alive!

She didn't say anything, only showed her fear.

But before the video ended, text appeared at the bottom of the screen.

I have my next victim in sight.

CHAPTER
TWENTY-SIX

PIPER AND BEAR had sent the video to Agent Townsend.

But Piper couldn't stop replaying the images of her friend.

The video hadn't revealed anything about Julie's whereabouts.

The footage had been grainy and low quality. Darkness had surrounded Julie, and even with Piper's skills, she hadn't been able to tell if Julie was simply in a dark room or in a tunnel.

Piper was certain the killer had planned it that way.

An hour later, Bear rose. "I want to talk to my neighbors, see if they've seen anyone lingering around my house."

"You have neighbors?"

"I suppose that's what you'd call them."

"How many neighbors do you have?"

"A retired couple owns some property about two miles to the east. There are also a couple of hunting cabins and one vacation home. That's about all there is on this mountain. Would you like to come with me?"

Piper stood. "I'd love to. It beats sitting here and thinking about things."

She'd given him space since their last conversation. She knew Bear needed to think. So, they'd both sat at the kitchen table, working on their own projects quietly.

But the idea of getting out of the house to check on something?

It had her vote.

She and Bear bundled up against the winter weather and went out to his truck.

They headed down the mountain road toward Bear's neighbors.

The hunting cabins were closed up for the winter, and no one occupied the vacation home.

The retired couple was at their house, but they hadn't seen anything.

Finally, they pulled up to the last house, a log cabin nestled in the middle of thick woods.

Piper stared at it.

The place looked abandoned, with its crooked porch, with mold growing on the sides, with the ripped screens over the dirty windows. A crude wooden sign with the words "Deertail Hollow" hung above the door.

A knot formed between Bear's eyes. "I heard someone bought this place a few months back."

Something about the place made her guard go up. This place didn't look like it had been lived in for years.

"There's probably no one here, but let me make sure." Bear took off his seatbelt and grasped the door handle.

"I don't think that's a good idea. This place looks like bad news."

"It's not haunted, if that's what you think."

"No, but it looks like somewhere bad things happen."

"How about this? You stay here, and I'll go up."

Piper's heart pounded in her ears. "I appreciate that you're trying to protect me, but—"

"I'll leave the truck keys in the ignition. Lock the doors and if anything happens—"

Before Bear could finish, the front door to the cabin slowly opened.

They both stared at it, waiting to see who would appear . . .

————

The man who stepped onto the porch looked normal. Too normal almost.

He was on the shorter side, with thinning hair, large ears, and saggy jowls. A heavy coat covered his shoulders and well-used work boots made the man seem blue-collar.

Bear released his breath.

"If it isn't Bear Colson." The man stepped closer.

Bear exchanged a look with Piper before climbing from his truck and stepping toward the man. "I am. You must be . . ."

"Dell. You probably don't remember this, but I met you back when you were a little thing." He held his hand to his waist to indicate that Bear had just been a child.

"How did we meet?" Bear asked.

Piper scrambled around the truck to join them.

The woman was curious. Of course, she wasn't going to simply sit in the truck and wait for Bear to recap their conversation. It wasn't in her nature.

"I was actually friends with your father," Dell said. "We met at church and went fishing together a few times. I moved away, so I wasn't here when he was arrested. I just bought this place as a hunting cabin so I could reconnect with the area. For the record, I never thought your father was guilty. I thought it was a shame when he went to prison. I really did."

"I appreciate that."

"I was glad to hear he'll be coming home soon. That's not just a rumor, right?"

"That's the plan." Bear nodded slowly.

"Well, that's good news. He deserves all the happiness." Dell paused and tilted his head. "So, what brings you out this way?"

"We won't take much of your time," Bear said. "This is my friend, Piper, by the way. We just have a couple of questions."

"Sure." Dell nodded behind him. "Would you like to come inside? There's a nip in the air out here."

"I think we're fine." Bear glanced at Piper.

She nodded. "I'm good."

Dell shrugged. "Have it your way. What do you need to know?"

Bear shifted, his boots crinkling the dry leaves beneath him. "Have you seen anyone out in these woods? Specifically, anyone near my property?"

Dell didn't have to think about it for very long. "As a matter of fact, I have. Just yesterday, I saw a man putting up some trail cams."

Bear straightened, unsure if he'd heard correctly. "You did?"

Dell tugged on his jacket sleeves before crossing his arms. "Sure did. Didn't think anything of it. So many people out here let friends use their property for hunting. Thought you might also."

Bear's heart beat faster. "Can you describe this man?"

"Not well." Dell frowned and he stared in the distance as if trying to re-create the moment. "He was pretty far away and wearing camo with an orange hat. He was whistling."

"Was he whistling a certain tune?" Piper asked.

"No, I mean, he wore a whistle and kept blowing it every so often. Kind of strange, but to each their own." He shrugged. "But that's it. I'm sorry I can't be more help."

"No, that's great. Thank you. If you see someone again, can you give me a call?" Bear handed him a card.

"Of course. And if you ever need anything, just reach out to me . . . neighbor."

At least Dell had offered them *something*.

But how would they find the man with the whistle who'd installed trail cams?

CHAPTER
TWENTY-SEVEN

"I KNOW you're disappointed that he didn't know more," Piper said once she and Bear were back in his truck. "I'm sorry."

He shrugged. "It is what it is."

"Listen, why don't we grab some lunch? It will be my treat. I think we could both use a change of scenery."

"Lunch would be good."

A ray of hope flooded her. Maybe they could turn this around and this discouragement would only be temporary. But this case was clearly wearing on both of them.

"How much time until your next class?" Piper asked.

Bear glanced at his watch. "Three hours."

"We'll be back in plenty of time. I heard about a place here in town, a restaurant called The Garage."

"I've heard it's supposed to be good. I'm in."

With that settled, they took off down the road.

"Dell seemed nice," Piper said.

He nodded. "I don't remember him, although I may have heard his name before."

"At least, now you know one of your neighbors."

"At least."

Piper glanced at the trees surrounding them as they headed down the road. "Do you ever get lonely living out here by yourself?"

"Not really. I like the solitude." He glanced at her. "You live in Lexington, near downtown. Isn't that what you told me?"

"It is."

"Is that what you like? Being surrounded by people and busyness all the time?"

Piper thought about it a moment before shrugging. "I do like being around people. But I like quiet also. I guess it's just finding the balance in all of it."

"You ever want to get your old job back? Work for the police department again?"

For some reason, Bear's question startled her. Piper quickly shrugged as she remembered her earlier phone call with Phil. She had some decisions to make.

"Sometimes, I like being my own boss. Other times, I like the security of having a consistent paycheck. Money hasn't been coming in as readily as I'd hoped. As I've mentioned before, paying my bills has been a bit of a struggle."

"It's not easy striking out on your own."

She shrugged. "Honestly, I didn't have much of a choice. No one wants to hire me after . . . well, it's going to take a lot of work to earn back my reputation."

"Restoration *is* possible, though."

She threw him a grateful smile, appreciating his encouragement. Because honestly . . . sometimes she wondered if she was just spinning her wheels. Maybe what had happened had caused irreversible damage and there was no going back.

Wedding photography was seeming more tempting all the time.

But that wasn't what got her blood pumping.

Helping solve crimes did.

Piper and Bear pulled up to the restaurant just in time. Maybe eating would be the perfect distraction for Piper from her otherwise heavy thoughts.

Bear took a bite of his salmon, thankful that Piper had suggested going out to eat. Getting some fresh air and out of his house had done his mind some good. Plus, The Garage was nice.

True to its name, the place had once been a garage, and evidence of that had been used as decorations. The pleasant scent of garlic and onions filled the air of the American-themed restaurant.

But there was still so much to think about. He needed to stay focused.

"I want to go in those old tunnels," Piper announced as she stabbed a piece of smothered chicken on her plate. "I want to see for myself. I need to know Julie's not inside one."

Bear blinked and stared at her a moment. "I thought we already established that wasn't a good idea."

"I know the FBI and professionals are searching the mine. But I just can't stop thinking that Julie could be inside one of the tunnels. What if she's there and I didn't do everything in my power to find her?"

"Why don't you think long and hard about this first? Those tunnels are nothing to be messed with."

"I know." Piper swallowed hard. "Believe me, I know. I just wonder if law enforcement has truly checked all of them. I feel so guilty knowing that I'm out here having this nice lunch with this great guy"

—she cleared her throat as if she hadn't meant to say that—"while my friend could be suffering. Yet I don't know how to fix it."

"Sometimes there's not anything we can do to fix things. We just have to accept them for what they are."

Bear knew there was a subtext to his words. For years, Bear had tried to fix the situation with his family to no avail. In order to have peace within himself, he'd simply come to terms with reality instead of trying to change things beyond his control.

Bear glanced up as two people walked past his table.

He felt tension pull across his chest.

"Everything okay?" Piper followed his gaze.

"That's Frank and Liz Emerson. The GSK killed their daughter, Emily. She was in a 'bike accident' while riding near the lake. Anyway, for the past fifteen years, the two of them have hurled insults at me whenever they see me."

"I'm sorry."

He shrugged. "It is what it is."

Would they treat Bear differently now knowing that someone else had been arrested and his dad cleared?

Based on the glare they gave him as they walked past, probably not.

It was one of the side effects of his father being an accused serial killer. Some people instantly thought Bear was a bad guy also or he should be punished for his father's sins.

Bear looked away from them, unwilling to give them the satisfaction of a reaction.

He didn't expect an apology. But it would be nice if people would finally just let go of the judgments they'd held onto for so long.

He and Piper finished eating, and Piper went to pay the bill. Bear took it from her before she could.

"I insist," he told her, pulling out his wallet.

"But—"

"No buts. Besides, you paid at the diner. It's my turn."

She opened her mouth as if to argue but then shut it and nodded. "Fine. But just let it be noted that this wasn't my idea."

A few minutes later as they stepped outside, Piper grabbed his arm and pointed to someone in the distance. "Look who just pulled into town."

CHAPTER
TWENTY-EIGHT

"WHO IS IT?" Bear followed her gaze.

Piper felt her throat squeeze as she stared at the plump woman with short auburn hair and the tall, painfully thin man with her. "It's Julie's parents."

All she could think about was the verbal lashing Luna's mom had given her. A lashing that Piper deserved.

Would she get lambasted again? Would Julie's parents march up to her and let everyone within listening distance know that it was her fault Julie had been abducted? Would TV cameras be rolling nearby, only adding to her humiliation?

She froze a moment, unsure what she should do.

Piper wanted to run to Mr. and Mrs. Anderson. To hug them. To tell them how horrible she felt about this situation.

Emotionally, Piper wasn't sure she could handle another confrontation.

Before she could decide, Julie's mom looked up and spotted Piper.

The next instant, she rushed across the sidewalk.

Piper braced herself for whatever would happen next.

"Oh, Piper . . ." Julie's mom threw her arms around Piper.

It took a couple of seconds for Piper's shock to wear off, but then she hugged Julie's mom too. "I'm so sorry."

Julie's mom wiped beneath her eyes. "Have you heard anything else? The FBI said something about a video . . ."

Piper shook her head. "I've been doing everything I can to find Julie. But there's been nothing so far."

Mrs. Anderson sniffled and wiped under her eyes again. Her husband joined her and put a hand on his wife's shoulder. That familiar look of grief was also on his face—the hollow eyes, robotic motions, lackluster expressions.

"We have to go talk to the FBI right now," she said.

"Of course."

As her husband ushered her back to the sheriff's office, guilt pummeled Piper.

She wished again that killer had taken her and not her friend.

She needed to figure out where Julie was.

Even if it cost her everything . . .

———

Before Bear reached his truck, he paused by a sign on a community bulletin board.

"What is it?" Piper asked.

"There's a pickleball tournament today."

She grunted. "It seems too cold to have that."

"Pickleball players take the sport very seriously. If it's not raining or snowing, they're out there."

She stared up at him. "Are you hinting that you want to play?"

He let out a chuckle. "No, sorry. I wasn't being clear. This event is through Parks and Rec."

Realization washed over her. "Which Ted Russo is in charge of . . ."

"Exactly."

"Do you think he's at the tournament?"

"I think there's a good chance he will be."

Piper nodded slowly. "I'd love to see this guy

with my own eyes, see what kind of feeling I get from him."

Bear nodded toward a street in the distance. "The tournament is taking place just a few blocks over. We can walk."

"Perfect."

Bear offered his arm, and Piper slipped her hand into the crook of his elbow.

It felt natural for them to walk this close, to enjoy this kind of comfortableness around each other.

He shouldn't get used to it, though.

Piper wouldn't be in town forever. Both of them had enough baggage in their pasts to fill a container ship. Yet another part of him felt hopeful.

He connected with Piper intellectually. Their personalities meshed. And she was so darn beautiful.

It didn't matter right now. Right now, he just needed to concentrate on figuring out where Julie was. Her safety was the most pressing concern.

A few moments later, they paused at the pickle-ball court that had been installed at the community center a few years ago. A surprisingly large crowd had gathered to watch.

Most of the participants were seniors. Fog Lake had become a popular retirement destination in the past decade. But with the combined elements of ping-pong, badminton, and tennis, the sport appealed to people of all ages.

"Maybe you and I should try this sometime," Piper muttered as she lingered close to the chain-link fence surrounding the court. "It looks fun."

At once, Bear had an image of being older, in his later years of life. He pictured Piper by his side, sharing in adventures together.

The idea was very appealing.

Too appealing.

A familiar face distracted him from his thoughts. "There he is."

Piper straightened. "Ted Russo?"

Bear nodded. "The one and only."

CHAPTER
TWENTY-NINE

PIPER WATCHED TED RUSSO.

She'd seen the man's picture online, but, in person, he seemed so unassuming.

He was of medium height and build. He had thick, dark hair that seemed to defy his age, which she guessed to be near sixty. He wore thick glasses that were now trendy, but she had a feeling he wasn't trying to keep up with styles. It was probably the same kind of glasses he'd worn for decades.

He wore black track pants with a matching zip-up hoodie, white sneakers, and a whistle around his neck.

A whistle?

She sucked in a breath.

Was that a coincidence? Dell had said the man he'd seen had a whistle.

Piper continued to watch while Ted monitored the pickleball tournament as if the event were his baby.

Could that unassuming man really be a killer? He looked so normal, so harmless. She thought she remembered Townsend saying he'd brought the man in for questioning also. If that was the case, Ted certainly didn't seem shaken up about it.

Was that because his conscience was clear and he had nothing to be ashamed of?

Or was it because he was a great actor?

"What do you think?" Bear leaned close and whispered.

A shiver ran through her. This time, it wasn't a shiver of fear. It was a shiver of excitement at feeling Bear's breath brush her ear.

Why was she letting the man have this kind of effect on her?

Piper wasn't sure she was "letting" anything happen. The fact of the matter was that it was just happening, with or without her consent.

She shoved those thoughts aside.

"He seems so . . . ordinary," she muttered.

"I agree. He's a perfectly likable guy."

"And the only reason he was a suspect was because he liked to jog with a GoPro, and, while doing so, he encountered a potential victim?" That didn't add up in Piper's mind.

"It's true. The evidence for the entire case was flimsy at best—even for my dad."

She shook her head. "Everyone was just desperate to put someone behind bars, weren't they?"

"Yeah, you can say that again."

And that was exactly what Piper didn't want to happen again. She didn't want to needlessly point fingers.

But she did need some answers.

Just as the thought went through her head, Ted strode toward them, a smile plastered on his face.

"If it isn't Bear Colson." Ted paused in front of them. "I haven't seen you around in a while. Not since I ran into you hiking last summer."

Bear's gaze darkened. "That's right. Mt. Sterling was quite the hike, wasn't it?"

The same smile remained plastered on Ted's face. "It sure was." Ted's gaze turned to Piper. "And who's this?"

"This is my friend, Piper. She's visiting right now. Piper, this is Ted."

"Pleasure to meet you." He extended his hand.

After a moment of hesitation, Piper shook it. But the fact that his skin felt clammy even in this cold weather left her feeling uneasy.

She glanced at his other hand, searching for a scar there. But it was nearly impossible to tell from this angle. Besides, it could have faded with time.

Still, as she stared, she didn't think she saw any marks.

"Question," Bear started. "Your dad used to work at the mine, didn't he?"

"He sure did. Retired from there right before it closed. I still remember him being paid in company script."

"Company script?" Piper asked.

"Oh, yes. The mine owners—they were mercenaries. They set up their own store, marked up the items, and made their employees buy from 'the company.' If they were caught buying anywhere else, it was means for being fired. Those were some crazy times."

"It sounds like it," Piper said. "You said the owners were mercenaries?"

Ted shrugged. "Maybe that's not the right choice of word. But OJ was as cold as ice. He lived in the biggest house at the top of the mountain, almost like he thought he was a king looking over his domain."

"And his brother?" Bear asked. "OD?"

"OD was nice—OJ's total opposite. Those two hated each other. I guess the only reason OJ hired OD was because his dad told him to. I always wondered whatever happened to those two."

Maybe Piper would dig a little more into them when she got back to Bear's.

"Anyway . . . it's good to see everyone carrying on as if things were normal, isn't it?" Ted turned back to the tournament.

"You mean, because of everything that's happening in this town?" Bear clarified.

"That's right." Ted raised his whistle and yelled something about a technicality before turning back to them. "I just can't believe this keeps going on and on. It's crazy, isn't it? It's like there's a whole network of sick people who just want to haunt this town, like they're drawn here or something."

A chill washed through Piper.

He was absolutely right.

The question was: was Ted one of those sick people?

———

Bear and Piper were quiet for much of the ride back to his house.

He had to teach again in forty minutes. But then, after that, he'd help Piper however he could. The last thing he wanted was for her to set out on her own to find answers.

Too much was on the line for her to do that, but she was just stubborn enough to consider the idea.

"I don't want to leave until Julie is found," Piper suddenly blurted.

Bear glanced at her, nearly startled at her random thought. "Of course. You can stay as long as necessary."

"I hate to impose. I just . . . I know you didn't plan on any of this and—"

"You're not imposing. The house is plenty big enough for both of us. And having some company . . . it's nice." Especially having Piper as company. She was spirited but smart, driven yet compassionate.

No one had caught his eye in a long time. But there was something different about Piper.

He didn't tell her that, though.

Instead, he reminded himself to keep his distance. The last thing he wanted was to get his heart broken —again.

"Thank you." Piper sent him a grateful look. "I really appreciate all you've done."

"I'm just as involved in this case as you are. My dad's name is on the line, my family's reputation. My brother and sister will be devastated if this doesn't come to an end."

"But not you?"

He felt Piper's gaze on him. "I will be too. But I

mostly just worry about my siblings. I've seen them lose everything once. I don't ever want to see that again."

Bear turned up the lane leading to his home. But he pressed on his brakes when he saw someone dart behind his house.

Someone was here.

Someone uninvited.

"Stay here!" he rushed.

He was going to catch this guy and find out exactly what was going on.

Bear threw his truck into Park, opened the door, and took off.

CHAPTER
THIRTY

PIPER SUCKED in a breath when she saw Bear storm away.

Someone was behind his property, weren't they?

She thought she'd seen movement in the distance. But, before she could comprehend what was going on, Bear had jumped into action.

She sat glued in her seat as she waited to see what would happen.

Should she get out and help?

Piper wanted to.

But she knew there was very little she could do.

Still, her heart pounded in her ears as she waited to see what the outcome would be.

Was that the killer lingering on the back of the property? Had he come to plant more cameras or other surprises?

Dear Lord . . . watch over Bear. Please.

Her gaze remained latched on the scene in front of her.

At any minute, she expected to see someone appear. She needed some kind of answer.

Or she would get out of this truck and go find her own answers.

The minutes seemed to crawl by. Should she call 911? By the time anyone got here it would be too late.

Piper could hardly breathe as she waited.

Finally, Bear rounded the corner of his house, holding a man up by his shirt.

Piper stared at the stranger with the fringe of dark hair around his head. His slight build.

Was that the Understudy?

If so, she hadn't expected him to look so unassuming.

She waited for only a moment before popping out of the truck and rushing toward him. As capable as Bear was, he might need her help. She couldn't just sit and watch.

As she got closer, the man's face became clearer.

She'd seen him before.

Wait . . . was that . . . ?

"Frank Emerson," Bear mumbled.

That's right. The man they'd seen in the restaurant. The one whose daughter had been killed by the GSK.

"He was spray-painting a message on the back of my house," Bear continued. "The word 'Killer,' to be exact."

Piper's gaze flickered back to Frank. The momentary fear she'd seen on his features turned to rage.

"I don't believe your dad is innocent," Frank growled, practically baring his teeth as he struggled against Bear's hold. "He had something to do with my daughter's death."

"Even if that's true, why make Bear pay?" Piper asked. "He didn't do anything."

"When someone's child suffers, so do the parents. You can't imagine what my wife and I have been through . . . now I want to make James Colson hurt like I've been hurt." Spittle flew from Frank's mouth as he stared at Bear.

"They've arrested someone else for the murders," Piper reminded him.

"Ralph obviously wasn't working alone!"

"Even if Ralph Burgess was working with someone, James Colson can't be responsible for what's happened over the past few days," Piper said. "He's been in jail."

"Someone needs to pay!" Frank's voice cracked as he sucked in raspy breaths.

As a tear ran down the man's face, Bear loosened his hold on him.

Frank was obviously grieving . . . deeply.

Piper's heart panged with compassion toward the man. He'd gone through something terrible. And though his anger toward Bear was misplaced, Piper couldn't help but feel sorry for him.

After a moment of hesitation, Piper stepped forward and placed her hand on his shoulder. "I'm really sorry for your loss. I can't imagine what you've been through."

"I miss her so much." His shoulders hunched. "Every day. People said it was going to get easier . . . but it hasn't."

Sobs wracked Frank's body as his hands covered his face.

"Grief is a terrible thing, but it also means that you loved deeply." Piper kept her voice gentle. "There's no shame in that. But Bear is just as much a victim here as you are. He's innocent and grieving also. You can't blame him for something he didn't do."

Frank shook his head as he squeezed the skin between his eyes. "I'm sorry. You're right. It's not your fault. I . . . I just need this to end. I need to make someone pay."

"Revenge doesn't feel as good as you might

think," Bear said quietly. "I wanted to make people pay for a long time also. It wasn't until I let go of that and realized I couldn't change the past that I felt like I could truly begin to live."

Frank stared at him a moment, emotions wavering in his gaze.

Finally, he shook his head, the motion heavy and burdened. "I shouldn't have blamed you. I just . . . I just want someone to pay, to suffer like I have. I'll come back and wash off that spray paint."

"I'll take care of it," Bear said quietly. "Why don't you get home before your wife wonders where you went?"

Frank nodded, still visibly shaken, with his hollow gaze and trembling limbs. "You . . . won't tell her what I did or call the cops?"

"I don't believe that will be necessary," Bear said.

"Thank you . . . and I'm sorry. I was talking to Harry earlier today and—"

"Harry Simpkins?" Bear interrupted.

"Yes, Harry Simpkins. You know his wife died not too long ago? We were talking about grief, and it made everything feel fresh again. And then when I saw you . . ."

Bear placed his hand on the grieving man's shoulder. "All is forgiven."

Bear and Piper walked him behind the house to

where his sedan was parked. They waited until Frank pulled away before they looked at each other.

She and Bear had talked about it before, talked about how a change in the killer's MO could be indicative of a change in his life.

Did that make Harry even more of a suspect? Had his wife's death awakened something in him?

Yet he had an alibi for the time when Julie had been abducted . . .

When Piper glanced back at Bear's house, she saw "Killer" staining the stone wall, the paint red and dripping.

She held back a frown at the sight of it.

How many more innocent people would have to suffer at the hands of this killer?

This monster had already caused too much pain.

He needed to be stopped before more lives were ruined.

———————

After Bear taught his class, he did a quick internet search and found what he was looking for: several videos of three college kids exploring the North Elk Ridge Mine system.

He'd heard thrill seekers liked to find abandoned

places, post videos of them on social media, and exploit them for as many views as possible.

But that wasn't what Bear found interesting.

It was the viewpoint he'd gotten of the mine system. The teens hadn't explored the tunnel where the human remains were found. At least, if they had, they hadn't seen the bones or they'd assumed they were from a dead animal. But they had covered quite a bit of distance in the tunnels.

This information could be very helpful.

He went downstairs to share the update with Piper. But when he saw her sitting with a laptop in her lap and a frown on her face, he knew something was wrong.

Piper pulled her gaze away from the screen, but only for a moment. "Bear, you'll never believe this. On Monday, when I went to the mine, I took several pictures. I didn't even think to look at them because I figured, at that point, it didn't really matter."

"Okay . . ." Bear waited to see where she was going with this, his pulse thumping in his ears. Whatever she'd discovered, she seemed excited.

"I decided to load them onto my computer so I could study them. When I did, I caught a glimpse of this." She clicked on one of the photos, and a picture of the front of the mine came into view.

No one was in the photo; it was only the mine entrance.

"I'm not sure what you're getting at . . ." Bear murmured, glancing at Piper and wondering what he was missing.

"It doesn't seem like anything at first, right?" Her voice lilted with excitement. "But then I began playing with some filters on the photos. Different filters and contrasts can allow you to see things in pictures that you miss at first glance."

"Okay . . ." Based on her tone, she'd discovered something noteworthy.

"Take a look at this." Piper enlarged the picture showing the east tunnel of the mine.

A dark hole stared back.

"It doesn't look like much now. But once I change the contrast . . ." Piper hit several keys.

As she did, the darkness faded slightly.

And at the side of the tunnel, Bear could barely make out the image of . . . a man.

His heart pounded harder as he realized what he was looking at.

"The Understudy . . ." Bear muttered.

"Exactly." Piper smacked her hand against her thigh. "I can't be sure, but it almost looks like he's wearing night vision goggles, doesn't it?"

Bear leaned in closer for a better look. "You're right. It does."

A chill washed through him at the sight of it. The image . . . it was eerie.

"If Luna and I hadn't gone down that other tunnel, he might have grabbed all of us," Piper continued. "Julie waited for us at the split. This guy must have seen his opportunity to grab her. He knocked her out with that spray so we couldn't hear anything. Then he carried her down the tunnel before we even knew anything was happening."

"That sounds accurate."

Piper glanced at him. "I'm not sure if that's going to help us solve anything or not. But at least it's something."

"You're right. It gives us a better idea of what was going on. This guy must have been keeping an eye on the footage, probably from a cell phone or computer. From the time you passed the first trail cam until you reached the tunnel probably took you about an hour, if I had to guess."

"I didn't even notice them, but the whole hike took an hour and thirty minutes or so."

"So, wherever this guy was, whatever he was doing, he was able to drop everything and make it inside that tunnel, most likely on foot," Bear continued. "You would have heard an ORV."

"Right."

Bear sighed and leaned back. "This just keeps getting crazier by the moment."

"Yes, it seems to, doesn't it? We have to find a way to stop all this. I want to make a list of every mine entrance we can find out about," Piper said. "Maybe that will provide us with some of the answers we've been looking for."

CHAPTER
THIRTY-ONE

PIPER MARKED another place on the map.

"This is what we have so far." She pushed her printout across the table toward Bear. "Twelve different openings located all throughout the mountain and beyond."

Bear stared at the map, his jaw twitching. "That's pretty crazy to think about."

"Most of them are close to the mining entrance—relatively speaking, at least. I'd say within a quarter of a mile. But several branch out farther, including the one by the Falling Timbers store—the one we saw."

"Which was a vertical shaft and probably impossible to enter through." Bear shifted. "Speaking of which, Sheriff Wilder told me those footsteps we saw outside the mine were left by some park rangers who'd been out there. The FBI has been examining each of the other entrances as they've been searching for Julie."

"That's comforting to know."

Bear pointed to the map. "This is North Elk Ridge Mountain, where the mine is located. The mountain where I live is here." He pointed beside North Elk Ridge. "This is Homestead Knob. This ridge connects them."

"Interesting." Piper stared at the map again, at all the Xs she'd marked.

Many of the entrances were on public land that no one owned. Some of the entrances were vertical shafts, mostly placed there to allow the mine—and the people inside—to breathe.

But, still, looking at the layout like she did now, it seemed nearly impossible for someone to get from Fog Lake and into that tunnel in time to grab Julie so quickly. There had to be other entrances they were missing. Unless the killer just happened to be in the mine for some other reason at the time they'd arrived, which was highly unlikely.

"This is going to help us out," Bear muttered. "I just got a photo of an old map of the mine from someone I used to go to church with. His daughter scanned it for him and sent it over."

"That's great."

Bear pulled it up, and Piper leaned closer for a better look. Several of the mine entrances were marked.

Piper compared this map to the one she'd started.

Then she paused at one of the marked entrances. "Bear . . ."

"What is it?"

"This entrance . . . if I'm not mistaken, it's on your property."

————

"We can't go looking for it right now," Bear insisted as he studied Piper's face and saw the gears in her brain turning. "It's already dark outside. It's too late."

She frowned and stared at the map. "You're right. But you're saying you had no idea it was there?"

"I have a lot of acres here. I've explored them. I know where a few caves are, but they're small ones that don't lead anywhere. I've never seen this mine entrance. You really think this is significant?" Bear studied her face.

"I don't know what's significant. Things just aren't adding up, and I desperately want answers. I want to go check this out."

"I don't blame you. But we need to be careful—and we need to let the FBI know what we're doing."

She nodded. "I agree."

Bear released his breath. At least there was that.

"One other thing." Piper tapped several keys on her computer. "I've been trying to research OJ and OD to see if we might be able to set up a phone call or something. But thirty years ago, there wasn't as much online about people. The brothers have mostly stayed off the radar since the mine closed."

"Were you able to find out anything about them?" Bear asked.

She showed him a picture. "Only this grainy photo of the two of them."

Bear looked closer to study it before shaking his head. "You're right. It's hard to tell anything from that."

"I'm going to keep looking." She let out a long breath. "Okay, back to that mine entrance. How about we go first thing in the morning? Do you teach tomorrow?"

"Not until the afternoon."

"Perfect then. We have a plan."

Bear stared at her another moment. Did they have a plan? Would journeying into the mine prove anything?

He wasn't sure.

But they could at least look for footprints, and he knew Piper wouldn't stop until her curiosity was satisfied.

CHAPTER
THIRTY-TWO

MY BOSS IS GOING on and on about things I don't care about.

I don't want to be here for this early morning meeting.

But my job pays my bills.

So I stay. And pretend to listen.

None of the people around me realize my splendor, realize who I am. They think I'm weak. Passive.

Maybe they'll always think that.

Maybe they'll never truly know what I'm capable of.

It's better that way.

That way I am free to do what I crave.

These fools make it easier.

My last kill was almost too easy.

I need more.

I can't seem to stop myself.

I don't *want* to stop myself.

I needed to make my mark.

So, I did.

And now I'm waiting.

These peons who are investigating always take too long to discover my clues. They think they're so smart.

They're not.

But there are two people that make me nervous.

Bear Colson's and Piper Stephens' faces fill my mind.

I don't like being nervous.

My pencil snaps in half.

My coworker glances at me, and I offer a feeble smile. "Cheap things. I want to know why they won't buy Ticonderoga."

Lousy Larry, as I call him in my head, seems appeased and turns back to our boss.

My thoughts return to my current situation.

I'm never nervous, never show my guilt.

My mom had once looked at me, terror on her face when she realized I wasn't crying over my father's death. She asked me if I ever felt anything. I told her no, not really. Not grief, at least. I suppose I get excited.

What would psychologists call that?

It doesn't matter to me.

I finally got that woman to say something last night, to tell me what Piper was doing.

It's about time someone looked more closely at the crime-scene photos.

I mean, I thought it would be a given, right? What took these clowns so long?

But Piper has an eye for things like this. That's what Julie said.

Finally, a formidable foe.

Now it's starting to get fun.

She's playing right into my hands.

Walking into my trap.

Because once I silence Piper, no one will be left to stand in my way.

CHAPTER
THIRTY-THREE

BEAR WORKED out the next morning, just as always. He needed to burn off some of his stress.

And he was definitely feeling stressed when he thought about going into the old mine tunnels today.

The excursion could end very badly.

And how could he not have known about the one near his house? It seemed like something he would notice, but there were areas he hadn't explored, and he hadn't specifically been looking for a mine entrance.

He understood Piper's thought process. He understood her urgency to find her friend.

This was day four.

The likelihood that Julie was still alive . . . it grew less probable as more time passed.

And if this guy was keeping her in the old mine,

how long could she survive in those conditions? They were anything but ideal.

When he finished working out, he scrubbed away the word "Killer" from the back of his house. Afterward, he fed his chickens and then quickly showered and got ready. By the time he got back downstairs, he saw that Madison and Rebecca had stopped by with some pastries from The Busy Bean, and they were chatting away with Piper like they were all old friends.

He took a cautious step toward them. "Ladies . . ."

"Hey, big bro." Madison reached up and kissed his cheek. "We brought some treats by. I hope you don't mind."

"Of course not." He glanced at Piper and saw she seemed to fit right in.

Why did that bring him a small amount of delight?

"That was awfully nice of you." He picked up a raspberry danish and took a bite. "To what do we owe this honor?"

"I just wanted to check on you." Madison's voice turned serious. "I know you've had a lot going on. It seems like we're each taking turns."

"It does, doesn't it?"

"I also wanted to mention a possible coming

home party for Dad . . ."

And there it was . . . the real reason she'd come by. "Isaac mentioned that."

"I'm hoping you'll be onboard. It will really just be for family and maybe a couple of others."

He saw the hopeful look on his sister's face and knew he couldn't refuse. "I'm in."

She let out a squeal. "I'm so glad to hear that. I think it's important that Dad know he has a support system. The transition . . . it could be difficult."

"This whole town should be throwing him a party," Bear muttered.

"I think that might overwhelm him. But you're right. They should."

They munched on the pastries and drank some coffee for a few minutes before Madison changed the subject.

"So, what do you all have planned for today?" Madison turned to them.

Bear quickly exchanged a glance with Piper, who remained silent.

"We're going to keep researching," he answered. "Between Piper's eye for photography and my computer skills, we're hoping we can figure out something."

"I hope you're able to." Madison pressed her lips

together as if the situation pressed heavily on her mind.

Bear's expression mirrored hers. "Me too. Me too."

———

An hour later, Piper and Bear started across his property. At least it wasn't uncomfortably cold today like it had been a couple of days earlier.

Using a pin on her GPS, she and Bear trekked through the woods making small talk as they did so. As she walked, Piper reflected on her conversation with Madison and Rebecca.

Madison admitted she'd been targeted by a GSK copycat, and that's how she'd met Shane.

Then Rebecca had told her that she'd been the GSK's victim nine years ago, the survivor Bear had alluded to. She'd shared her story as Piper had listened. The woman was certainly to be admired. They both were.

No wonder the family had such a bond.

Finally, an hour and a half after they left, they stopped at the pinned location.

"I don't see anything," Piper murmured.

"Me neither." Bear glanced around before pacing toward a cluster of trees against the mountainside.

He peered behind them and let out a grunt. "It's there. Behind these trees."

Piper followed his gaze and frowned. "Nothing looks disturbed in the area. No one is using that entrance."

"No, they're not. These trees must have grown here after the mine closed."

She let out a sigh. She'd been hopeful that maybe this would provide some answers. But that didn't appear to be the case.

"Hey." Bear nudged her chin up. "I don't like that look. It's . . . defeat. You're always so optimistic."

"Sorry." Piper tried to pull herself together. "This was just my best lead and now . . ."

"It's gone."

She nodded. "Yeah, it's gone, I guess."

"We'll keep looking."

"We're running out of time."

"I know it seems that way. But we're doing every-thing we can."

"What if that's not enough?" Her voice broke.

The next instant, Bear pulled her into his arms. And she let him.

As much as Piper feared trusting someone else again, there was something about Bear that made her want to tear down her walls.

And he was so strong. She felt so protected when he was with her.

If only she could stay here all day and just enjoy this moment . . .

But that wasn't an option.

"I guess we should get back," she finally murmured.

Bear released her from his embrace. When he did, Piper glanced up and their gazes caught.

They were standing close. Probably too close.

Close enough that Piper could reach up on her tippy toes and—

No, she couldn't think like that.

But Bear . . . he was so amazing.

Did he feel the same way about her?

Based on the look in his eyes right now, Piper thought the answer was yes.

"Can I show you something before we head back?" Bear's voice pulled her out of her trance-like state.

"Show me something?"

"I think you'll like it. It won't take long."

She nodded, temporarily forgetting everything else she needed to do. "Okay. Sure."

Bear grinned—which made her answer all worth it.

"Okay then. Let's go."

CHAPTER
THIRTY-FOUR

BEAR COULDN'T GET the look in Piper's eyes out of his mind.

Did she feel something too?

He wasn't sure. But he did know that it was a good change of pace just to have some breathing room from this case. It would do them both a world of good to take their minds off it for a few minutes.

As they maneuvered over an especially rocky area, he took her hand to help her.

Neither of them let go, and Bear wasn't complaining.

"It's really peaceful out here. I mean, except for the serial killer . . ." Piper's voice faded.

"It is. I love this property."

"You said you've lived here several years. How did you even afford it? Wait. You don't have to answer that. That's a nosy question, isn't it? Sorry, I can't seem to help myself. My curiosity just keeps popping out."

Bear chuckled. "I'd rather you ask than assume things. If I don't want to answer, I won't."

"Good to know."

"And I don't mind answering your question. Right after high school, I helped this guy with construction. I lived in the room over his garage and saved as much money as I could. I also went to school in between working, and I graduated debt-free. As soon as I had enough money for a down payment and I found this land, I put an offer on it."

"Impressive."

Bear shrugged. "I don't know about that. But I knew I didn't have a support system to fall back on. If it was to be, it was up to me, as the saying goes."

"Your dad has to be proud of you."

Bear felt his mood darken. "I don't know about that."

"I know things are probably complicated between you. I can't even imagine."

Thoughts collided in his head, things he'd been wrestling with and trying to come to terms about. "I appreciate that. I don't want to dim Madison's excitement, but throwing a party for my dad is the last thing I want. The truth is he chose to protect his secret girlfriend over protecting his children. I'm not sure I can ever come to terms with that."

"Maybe he regrets it." Piper looked up at him, a hopeful look in her gaze.

"If he regretted it, he could have come forward at any time during these fifteen years and admitted the truth. He didn't."

"Ouch."

Before they could talk about it anymore, a noise sounded in the distance.

A roaring.

Piper froze, her eyes widening a moment as if she were afraid.

Bear squeezed her hand. "It's okay."

He tugged her forward. As they rounded a rock formation, a small waterfall came into sight.

Piper sucked in a breath. "That's beautiful."

"I thought you might like it," Bear told her.

"I do." She stared at the twenty-foot drop into the creek.

"Want to go closer?"

"Why not?"

Still holding hands, they climbed over rocks and ventured closer to the waterfall. An icy, fine mist sprayed their faces, but the milder day made it bearable.

A small ledge led around the waterfall, almost making it look like . . .

"Can you walk behind it?" Piper asked.

"I don't know. I've never tried." Bear glanced at her. "Want to find out?"

"Sure."

———

Piper had to admit she felt a thrill as she continued to grasp Bear's hand. She didn't want to read too much into it but holding hands with him felt natural.

He tested the path in front of them as they walked toward the waterfall. They had to hug the rock wall as they got closer, but then suddenly they were behind the falls. The water poured down in front of them, giving the space a magical feel.

"We did it!" Piper shouted, unable to resist a giggle.

"We did." Bear grinned as he leaned toward her.

As he did, their gazes caught.

Piper sucked in a breath.

There it was again.

That look in his eyes.

This man seemed to have stepped off the pages of her dreams and into her life.

"I really like you, Piper." His voice sounded low and rumbly.

"I . . . I like you too."

The next instant, his hand cupped behind her neck. His other hand tilted her head up.

Their gazes locked, and Piper couldn't look away from his striking green eyes.

He dipped his head down until their lips connected—slowly but confidently.

When she didn't back away, he moved in closer, kissed her more deeply. She leaned into him, forgetting every other kiss she'd ever experienced.

This was the only one that mattered. And it was definitely one she wouldn't forget.

As they pulled away, her heart soared.

But the feeling didn't last long.

When she glanced beyond Bear, she spotted an opening in the shadows of the small cavern behind the waterfall.

An opening that looked a lot like . . . a tunnel.

'

CHAPTER
THIRTY-FIVE

"WHAT IS IT?" Bear turned around expecting the worst.

"A passageway."

His eyes widened as he stepped closer to the opening. "Yes, it is."

Piper peered in behind him. "Do you think this connects with the mines?"

Bear remembered the other entrance's location and nodded slowly. "Based on what I've seen, I'd say there's a good chance that's correct. With the ridge connecting these two mountains, it makes sense."

Piper gripped his arm. "Bear . . . how close is this waterfall to any major roadway?"

He let out a breath. "State Route 52 doesn't run too far from here. Maybe a quarter mile."

"So, if someone knew this was here . . ."

"It would be an easy way to access the mines," he finished.

Piper stared into the tunnel. "Should we?"

Every part of him screamed no. But they were here, and it seemed a shame to leave without seeing if there was any evidence inside.

They stepped into the opening.

"We can't go far, just to be safe," he said. "In spaces like this, you never know where the ground may disappear and plunge you into a deep shaft."

"Noted," Piper said.

"Four people are ideal for exploring areas like these," Bear said. "Which reminds me, we forgot to tell Shane this morning that we were coming out this way to look for the mine entrance. No one knows we're here, which can also be a hazard."

"True." She stared into the space. "I'm just thinking this could be an easy way for someone to escape the mine. How far do you think we are away from the main entrance? Not traveling on roads. Just straight distance."

He let out another breath. "I'm going to guess a mile or so. Not very far, if roads weren't a choice."

She stored that fact away.

Bear held out his hand. "Come on. Just a few steps. That's all."

She swallowed the knot of fear in her throat and

stepped into the dark space, waiting for her eyes to adjust. Bear pulled out his flashlight and shone it around.

The beginning of the space looked like a cave. But as the light reached the back, old wood beams could be seen around the walls and ceiling.

Her heart pounded harder. They were onto something.

They took a couple more steps when she paused. "Bear, what's that?"

He knelt down and lifted something from the ground.

As he shone his light onto it, the breath left her lungs.

It was an Explorer Cadet badge.

Explorer Cadets . . . Ted Russo was in charge of them.

The two of them exchanged another look.

"We should call Shane right away," Bear said.

"Absolutely."

Bear took her hand. "Come on. Let's find a signal."

"Of course." She raised her camera. "But first, let me take a few photos."

————

When Bear and Piper emerged from the woods, they went straight to Bear's truck and took off. They tried to call Shane, but he didn't answer. They would keep trying.

In the meantime, they headed to Ted Russo's place.

Time wasn't on their side.

Several minutes later, they pulled up to Ted's house—a humble clapboard bungalow on the edge of downtown.

As they strode toward the door, it opened, and Shane emerged.

Surprise lit the FBI agent's gaze when he saw them there.

"What are you guys doing?" Shane paused on the porch, Ted lingering in the doorway behind him.

"We tried to call you, Shane." Bear nodded toward Ted, an icy tone to his voice. "I found an Explorer Cadet badge on my property—in an old mine tunnel. We came here to ask Ted Russo how it got there."

Shane turned toward Ted. "Care to explain?"

Ted's face paled, and he raised his hands in innocence. "It's true. I didn't think you'd mind, so I took a few of my Lion Cadets there to see the tunnel behind that waterfall. I heard it was there, and I wanted to see for myself."

"How did you hear it was there?" Shane asked.

"All the old timers here know. They talk about going there when they were teens." Ted sliced his hand through the air. "But that's all I did. I promise. We didn't go inside for any other reason."

Shane crossed his arms. "Have you been exploring these tunnels a lot?"

"No!" Ted answered quickly. "Only once. I swear."

Shane's gaze narrowed as if skeptical. "I'm going to need the names of the cadets who were with you."

"Of course. Anything." Ted paused, his gaze bouncing back and forth between all of them. "I'm not responsible for what's happening. You've got to believe me."

Shane pressed his lips together. "It's better if you don't leave town. Am I clear?"

Sweat beaded on the man's forehead. "Of course."

As the three of them walked back to their cars, Bear turned to Shane. "I really did try to call to give you the update."

"I saw that, but I was in the middle of talking to Ted. I was going to call you when I left."

"If you don't mind me asking, why are you here?" Bear turned back to Shane. "Did you find more evidence against Ted?"

Shane shrugged and paused near his SUV. "I can't say. But we're following every lead."

Bear figured that's what he would say. Shane had already shared more information than he was probably supposed to.

Piper turned toward him. "I've been meaning to ask—have you personally interrogated Ralph about any of this?"

"I have." Shane's jaw tightened. "He's not talking."

"We can't even be sure that the bodies we found in the mine are connected, can we?" Piper asked.

"No, not for sure. We're examining every angle right now." Shane nodded toward his SUV. "I'd love to talk more, but I've got to run."

Bear and Piper waited until they were back in Bear's truck before speaking again.

Piper had hoped that every clue they found would lead them closer to Julie. But every clue seemed to stall them instead. Right now, Ted Russo was at the top of her suspect list.

Were they really any closer to finding her friend now? She couldn't say with any certainty that they were.

"Don't get discouraged." Bear seemed to read her mind.

She tried to smile but couldn't. "I'm trying not to be. It just feels like this keeps going on and on."

"I know. But we're getting closer. I can feel it."

"I hope so."

Bear froze when his phone buzzed. As he glanced at the screen, he sucked in a breath.

Piper leaned closer. "What is it?"

"Someone just sent me a video." He clicked on a few things before pressing Play.

Piper peered at his screen, anxious to see what this could be.

Her eyes widened when she realized it was a reel of outtakes from the Understudy's murders.

The killer was trying to provoke them, wasn't he?

The only reason he would do that was because he thought he had the upper hand.

CHAPTER
THIRTY-SIX

BEAR COULDN'T TAKE his eyes off one of the victim's video clips.

The ones of Jen Allendale before she died.

These pieces of footage didn't make the final cut. Footage that included this monster pulling her out of the lake only to drop her back into the water over and over again. Footage of him talking to her in a mocking tone while she pleaded for her life.

This man was sick. And this video proved it.

It was almost set up like a blooper reel at the end of a comedy. He even included laugh tracks.

"He's taunting us," Piper said.

Bear nodded as he stared at the screen. "He's delighting in what he's getting away with. He feels untouchable."

"I agree. He's going to mess up sometime though. I just hope it's not too late before he does."

He wrapped his arm around her waist and pulled her close. "Me too. Because we know that he's already preparing to strike again."

"Yet he's holding onto Julie. I think. I *hope*. I still can't figure that out. I can't figure out why he would keep her alive. Don't get me wrong. I'm thankful. And you could be right. Maybe he originally kept her alive to get information. But at this point, I would assume that he would have all of that." She shook her head. "None of this makes any sense."

"We're going to figure this out," Bear assured her. "Somehow, someway we will."

———

Piper didn't miss the glances that Bear kept giving her as they sat in his living room. He was worried about her. But nothing made sense to her, and she didn't even know which end was up at this point.

At the height of the afternoon, tires crunching on gravel sounded outside Bear's house. A moment later, somebody knocked on the door, and Bear answered.

The voice she heard on the other side brought her to her feet.

She snapped out of her daze and stepped toward the door. "Luna?"

Piper could hardly believe her eyes. That was definitely Luna wearing some gray sweatpants, a tie-dye sweatshirt, and white sneakers. Her hair was twisted into a messy bun on top of her head, and oversized glasses adorned her face.

What was her intern—or former intern, she should say—doing here?

Luna glanced at her and stepped closer. "I'm sorry to show up unannounced like this. But I just couldn't stay in Lexington knowing that Julie is still out there somewhere."

"But your mom . . ."

"I told her what I was doing. My parents aren't happy with me right now, but they didn't try to stop me either. I am nineteen years old. I'm paying for college myself and living on my own. I feel like I should have some say in what I do."

Piper stared at her another moment, unsure what kind of advice she should give. On the other hand, she felt so worn-out and depleted that maybe she didn't have any good advice to offer.

"I think it's nice that you wanted to come," Piper finally said. "But I'm not sure what you can do. We've been working nonstop, but we haven't made very much progress. Julie is still out there somewhere, and we still have no idea who the Understudy is."

Luna frowned, crossed her arms, and leaned against the wall. "I was hoping that maybe there was a better update. I've been doing what I can from Lexington."

"I appreciate the fact that you're invested in this," Piper said. "What have you tried to do?"

"I set up a tip hotline website. Part of me felt like I should run it past you first, but then I figured . . . why not? It was something I wanted to do to see if it could help so I did it."

Piper perked up slightly. "A tip hotline? You mean to see if anyone saw anything?" She liked the idea of it, but the area where the crime had occurred was so secluded. What were the odds that someone had seen anything?

"I know it seems like a long shot. But I figured it couldn't hurt. Maybe someone saw a vehicle parked somewhere nearby. Or maybe someone saw somebody entering the woods? Besides, you remember that one killer that was caught? Walter Gomez, who also went by Jesus Centoreo? He was captured all because of a tip someone called in."

Bear stepped closer. "And what did you find out?"

"Most of what I've gotten hasn't been anything

noteworthy. Not even something I would report to the police. Someone in New Mexico claims she saw her. I even got one tip involving Elvis and aliens." Luna rolled her eyes. "But I'm still hopeful that something will come in that will help us find her."

"I think that's great that you're trying to do something." Piper patted her shoulder. "And I'm glad you came."

"Thanks." Luna pushed her hair behind her shoulder and glanced up almost shyly, reminding Piper that she was still young. Even though she was wicked smart, this girl had just graduated from high school less than two years ago.

"Listen." Bear stepped forward. "I feel like we could all benefit from getting out of the house for a while. I know they're having some food trucks and music down at the town square. What do you guys say we stop by for a visit and maybe listen to the scuttlebutt about town?"

Piper nodded, liking the sound of that. "It beats staying here and staring at the walls. Let's do that. Great idea."

CHAPTER
THIRTY-SEVEN

BEAR WASN'T sure what to think about Luna's presence here. But the college student seemed to want to help. A tip line was probably a long shot, but maybe it had made her feel better to know that she was doing something.

In the meantime, the heaviness of the situation was beginning to wear on them all. Finding Julie was all he and Piper had been able to think about all week. It had almost become their obsession. Yet they'd gotten nowhere, which could also lead to discouragement.

Maybe doing something to clear their heads would be the best medicine for them to find a solution.

Twenty minutes later, Bear pulled into the downtown area and found a parking space. The streets were more crowded than he'd thought they would be, but the day was nice. It shouldn't surprise him that people had come out to enjoy this. Eight food trucks had been set up in a U shape. Also, various artisans had set up tables to sell their handcrafted creations. A band performed on the stage in the distance, singing a popular cover song.

They climbed from his truck and began to tour the town square. As they did, the scents from the various food trucks filled the air.

Sizzling beef. Fried potatoes. Spicy chili.

"No matter what you want to eat, you should be able to find something here," Bear said.

Piper stepped closer to him. "This looks great. Good idea."

"I think I'm going to walk around and check out the various foods available if that's okay," Luna said. "I love food trucks."

"Go ahead," Piper said. "We'll catch up with you."

As soon as she walked away, Piper turned toward him. "That was unexpected."

Bear followed Luna with his gaze. "Yes, and I'm not sure what she's going to be able to do here. The last thing I want is more trouble."

"You mean trouble like her parents showing up and giving us an earful again?"

"That certainly wouldn't help the situation."

Piper let out a breath. "No, it wouldn't."

They began wandering the perimeter of the square and looking at the various food trucks.

"Can you eat from any of these? I know most of them probably serve beef."

He nodded at a couple of them. "I know some owners, and they know about my food allergy. They'll make sure to decontaminate everything so I shouldn't have any issues."

"That's nice they would do that. So, what are you leaning toward?"

His gaze perused the area and stopped at one truck—The Toasted Tortilla. "I'm thinking a chicken enchilada sounds really tasty."

"I was thinking Mexican sounded good too."

Just as they started toward the truck, the band began to play a new song.

Piper froze on the sidewalk and glanced around.

"What is it?" Bear asked.

"This song . . . it's by Third Eye Blind."

"That's the same song that the killer left playing in Lisa Moreno's CD player when it fell into the pool, right? 'Never Let You Go.'"

Piper nodded, her neck looking stiff. "I'm having trouble believing that this is a coincidence."

"Let's go find out." He took her hand and led her toward the stage area.

———

Piper hoped that she was simply being paranoid. That was the most likely scenario.

But the song they sang right now . . . she hadn't heard it in years. And that's what made her suspicious.

She and Bear stood at the base of the stage and listened to the band. As soon as the song was over, Bear stepped forward. "Excuse me . . . did somebody just request that song?"

The lead singer, a twenty-something man with bleached blond hair, leaned toward them and nodded. "They did actually. Why?"

"Do you know who it was?"

The singer glanced through the crowd before shrugging. "My manager just gave me a piece of paper with the song title written on it. I don't know who wrote it."

"Who's your manager?" Bear asked.

"That guy over there." The singer nodded toward a man with wire-rimmed glasses and long blond hair.

Piper took off toward the man, determined to get some answers.

Because if their suspicions were true, then that might mean that the killer was here right now. Watching them. That he'd somehow known that they would arrive, would hear that song, and make the connection.

"Excuse me," Bear called. "Can you tell me who requested that song 'Never Let You Go'?"

He turned to them and looked annoyed for a brief second. "I don't know who requested it. They left the song title on the sound board along with a twenty-dollar donation. That's all I know."

Bear glanced at the sound tech. "So, no one saw anything?"

The tech shook his head. "No, man. Sorry."

Bear turned back to Piper, and they both shared the same expression.

Disgust.

But the feeling was immediately followed by fear.

If this guy was here right now, was he planning something?

And what if it involved one of them?

They needed to find Luna.

And they didn't have any time to waste.

CHAPTER
THIRTY-EIGHT

THEY CAUGHT UP WITH LUNA. She had gotten a falafel wrap with pickled vegetables.

Bear contemplated whether they should tell her about the song before deciding not to say anything. If Piper decided to do so, that was her choice. But for now, he just asked Luna to stay close considering everything that was going on.

Luna seemed to understand that and nodded. "Probably a good idea."

"How about we go get some tacos?" Piper asked, turning to Bear.

"Let's do that."

As they walked toward the truck, Bear glanced around, looking for anyone suspicious nearby.

But that was the thing. This guy probably didn't look suspicious. He probably blended right in.

When it was time for them to place their order, Bear reminded Danio, who owned the truck, about his meat allergy. Danio assured him that he would make sure there was no cross-contamination.

Bear paid and then they joined Luna as they waited for their order number to be called.

As Piper and Luna began chatting about a Wildcat basketball game, Bear studied everyone around him again.

It seemed like the whole town had come out for this event today. Maybe everyone was ready to thaw from the cold weekends they'd had lately. On the corner of Main Street, a memorial had been set up for Jen Allendale. An enlarged photo had been left there, and people surrounded it with flowers and stuffed animals.

Seeing it reminded Bear of the heartbreak of this situation.

He continued to study everyone around him.

Ted Russo was overseeing an outdoor "skating" rink that was actually a slippery floor where kids wore socks and slid around.

Harry Simpkins was also there talking to several friends and calling hello to people he knew as they passed by.

Even Anthony was out—and ordering food from the same taco truck Bear had.

But just because those men were here didn't mean that they were guilty of anything.

Bear let out a breath. He hated being suspicious of everyone. But how could he not be, considering everything that had happened?

Their order number was called, and Luna jumped up. "Let me get it for you. I want to get a better look at the cook. He was checking me out earlier."

Luna plastered on a smile as she approached the truck. She exchanged a few words with Colton, Danio's cook, before bringing their food to them and announcing that Colton was hot.

Behind that gaze hooded with grief was a regular college student thrown into an unimaginable situation. He fought a frown.

Bear quickly inspected his to make sure no red meat or dairy had been added. Then he took a bite.

A few minutes later, as sweat covered his brow, he knew something was wrong.

His throat began to tingle, and that's when he knew what was coming.

But it was too late to stop it.

His throat started swelling.

"Bear?" Piper looked up at him with wide eyes.

He couldn't respond to her.

Because he could no longer breathe.

———

As soon as Piper looked at Bear, she knew exactly what was happening.

"Where is your EpiPen?" she asked.

Somehow, despite the way he grasped his throat, he reached into his pocket and handed his keys to her and pointed toward the truck.

Without waiting another second, she darted across the town square to where he'd parked.

She didn't have a moment to waste.

She checked the middle console first, and when she didn't see it, she almost panicked. Bear was in no shape to tell her exactly where to find it.

Maybe she should have called 911 first.

But there was no time for that.

Where would he keep it?

She popped open the glove compartment.

She spotted it on top of some paperwork.

Hands shaking, Piper grabbed the EpiPen and darted back toward him.

By that time, a crowd had gathered. Bear sat on a bench but leaned over, gasping for air.

Quickly, Piper pulled the cap from the EpiPen and thrust the needle into his thigh.

Then she watched and waited.

Just as two paramedics rushed over, he dragged in a deep breath and leaned back.

Relief rushed through her until she nearly felt limp.

Bear was okay. Praise God he was okay.

Piper moved to the side as the paramedics came to look at him.

Luna sidled up next to her. "What just happened? Is he allergic to something?"

"He has a red meat and dairy allergy. I know he ordered chicken enchiladas and that Danio said he would make sure the area wasn't contaminated. I don't know what happened, but something must have been on that enchilada."

Luna's eyes widened. "That was scary."

Piper's hands were still shaking. "Tell me about it."

The paramedics told Bear he needed to go to the hospital, but Bear refused, insisting he would be fine. Piper promised to keep an eye on him.

As soon as the paramedics left, Piper sat beside him on the bench. The crowds seemed to disperse now that the excitement was over.

She placed a hand on his back and examined his face, looking for any signs that anything might still be wrong. He looked pale but otherwise okay.

"Thank you," he said with a raspy breath. "That will teach me to leave the EpiPen in my truck."

"I guess so. I'm just glad you're okay. Are you sure you don't want to go to the hospital?"

"I'll be fine."

She glanced at the enchilada on the ground where he had dropped it. Out of curiosity, she picked the paper container up, scooping it to make sure the food stayed inside, and used a fork to open the enchilada. It looked like chicken, tomatoes, and jalapenos were inside. Piper didn't see any beef or cheese or sour cream even.

So, what had caused that reaction?

As if he read her thoughts, Danio came over, concern obvious in the creases on his forehead.

"I was careful." He shook his head as if puzzled. "I cooked the enchilada myself. I made sure it wasn't cross-contaminated, just like I said. I changed gloves. Wiped down all the food prep surfaces. I don't know what happened."

Bear shook his head, obviously still out of sorts. "I don't either. I'm just glad that everything turned out okay."

"Me too," Danio said. "Me too."

AFTER EVERYONE HAD WANDERED AWAY, Bear turned toward Piper as they sat on a bench in the town square.

"My goal was to *not* draw attention to myself," Bear muttered.

"Well, you didn't do a very good job." Piper offered a soft smile.

He leaned toward her and planted a soft kiss on her forehead, grateful for her concern. "Thank you."

It almost looked like her cheeks flushed as she stared up at him. "Of course. Do you want to get back to your house now?"

His gaze wandered the crowd. There were so many people here. So many potential suspects.

He wasn't going to let this slow him down.

Although a certain question did remain in his head.

What if someone had planted red meat in his food? Or maybe some dairy?

He shook his head, not bothering to voice that concern aloud. The possibility seemed unlikely. Danio had made the enchilada, the server had passed the food through the window where Luna had picked it up and brought it to him.

There hadn't been enough time for anyone to put anything in his food. And not many people knew about his allergy anyway or how severe it was. For some people with alpha-gal, it took up to several hours for an allergic reaction. Bear's body seemed to react much more quickly.

No matter how it had happened, for now, he wanted to put the whole incident behind him.

On the stage in the distance, Bear heard an announcer talking to the crowds.

He immediately recognized the voice.

Arnie Siebert.

Another suspect was also here.

They definitely had more investigating to do before they left.

"Why don't we get closer and see what's going on onstage?" Bear suggested as he stood. "How's that sound to you, Luna?"

"I love small town festivals. I'm game."

"Then let's go."

Piper held Bear's hand as they walked through the crowd. Luna wandered off to look at various booths and to check out a couple of stores.

Bear's gaze remained on Arnie. The man had a flair for dramatics. And so did The Good Samaritan Killer and his Understudy. That's why those monsters wanted to broadcast what they did—so they could get all the praise and attention for seeming like good guys.

Could the Understudy be Arnie?

Bear couldn't rule the man out.

As he watched him, he felt someone step close behind him.

Bear's muscles tightened as he braced himself for whatever was about to happen next.

———

Piper felt Bear stiffen, and she turned, expecting danger.

Instead, Rex Morgan stood there with a friendly grin on his face.

"I thought I recognized you two." Rex stepped up beside them. "Good to see you out here."

Piper released the breath she hadn't even realized

she'd been holding. "I couldn't miss it. This is small-town life at its finest."

He adjusted the hat on his head. "I agree. It's good to have things to keep you busy. I thought I saw you two at the pickleball game yesterday too."

"Did you play?" Bear asked.

"I try not to miss it. Helps keep me in shape."

"Ted Russo seems to do a good job organizing it." Piper had chosen to bring him up on purpose, to see if Rex would take the bait and share anything about him.

She wasn't disappointed.

"Yes, Ted loves organizing these events. I knew his dad. He started out as my supervisor at the mine, but he retired after I'd only been there a few years."

"Is that right?" Piper stored away that information. It was just one more reason why the man might be guilty. "It's a small world, isn't it?"

"You can say that again. Ever since I talked to you, I keep running into people I used to work with at the mine. Some people don't like that kind of smallness. But I think it's refreshing."

Piper offered a smile.

Rex adjusted his hat once more before stepping away. "I need to get going, but you two enjoy yourselves."

Piper watched him turn and walk away before looking back at Bear.

They didn't have to say anything to know what the other was thinking.

Ted Russo was moving up higher on their suspect list.

CHAPTER
FORTY

AS DARKNESS BEGAN TO FALL, Bear, Piper, and Luna stayed around to listen to some more music. Bear's appetite was gone, and he had no intention of eating anything else here. He'd wait until he got home, no matter what his hunger pains might urge.

His allergic reaction had been a close call, and he was truly grateful for Piper's quick thinking when she'd grabbed his EpiPen.

But he couldn't stop thinking about how the killer was here. Bear wasn't ready to leave until he found more answers.

Several vendors had set up tables to sell jewelry, artwork, and photographs. After Bear, Piper, and Luna listened to some songs, they decided to cruise around the tables.

Bear recognized the woman who was selling some homemade soap. He paused by her table and smiled. "Hey there, Janet."

"Bear . . . good to see you."

"You too." He quickly introduced Janet to Piper and Luna.

"You know, I have to change something that I told you." Janet paused from straightening her jewelry displays. "I was going to call you later because I was thinking about it. I know I told you that Harry was in school all day Monday. But I got my days confused. We actually had a staff meeting on Monday because it was a teacher workday. And I seem to remember that he had to get up and leave early for something."

Bear's pulse quickened. So maybe they couldn't rule Harry Simpkins out either.

"That's good to know," he told her. "Thank you."

"Is everything okay?" She studied his face.

"Everything is fine. Thank you again for your help." The less she knew, the better.

It seemed like the suspect list was growing stronger, with each person having their own motive, means, and opportunity.

But how were they going to narrow it down to the person behind the crimes?

———

They stayed in downtown Fog Lake for another hour or so.

Before they walked back to Bear's truck, Luna ran to the bathroom.

Bear pulled Piper closer to his truck.

As he did, Piper's blood raced at his closeness.

"Thanks again for what you did back there," Bear murmured.

Instinctively, she reached her arms around his neck. "Of course."

"You're an amazing woman, Piper. I just want you to know that. I've known since the moment we first met."

She felt her cheeks heat. "Thanks. I think you're pretty amazing also."

He lowered his head until his lips met hers. Not just met hers.

Consumed hers.

The kiss swept her away until everything else disappeared. It was just her and Bear.

No hesitation.

No doubt.

No fear.

As he pulled back, she felt her heart racing and ran a hand across her tingling lips. "That was . . . surprising."

He pushed a strand of hair behind her ear as he

gazed at her, something deep and lingering in his gaze. "I've been wanting to kiss you all evening."

A grin stretched across her lips. "That makes me very happy to hear."

Before they could talk more, Luna appeared. "Ready to go?"

The moment was over too fast.

On the way back, Piper's mind raced.

She wanted to dwell on that kiss. To relive it. To relish it.

But other thoughts tried to invade the happy moment.

Thoughts of the Understudy. About who he could be. About how they would find him.

Could Harry Simpkins have left the staff meeting at school in order to grab Julie?

But Ted Russo's father had worked for the coal mine, which meant he might have inside information on how to navigate the tunnels.

Then there was Arnie . . . his personality matched the kind of person Piper saw in her mind as the bad guy. Someone who liked attention.

She still had so many questions.

Then there was the issue of Bear's food allergy. Piper wanted to believe it was just a mistake that he'd eaten something harmful.

But what if it wasn't?

Could someone have planted something in his food? Piper hadn't wanted to raise the possibility in front of Bear. But the question wouldn't leave her mind—especially since Anthony had been lingering nearby.

They got back to Bear's place, and he excused himself to grade his students' assignments.

As he did, Piper helped get Luna's bedroom ready. Bear had said she could stay for the night, and Luna had agreed. When they finished, they sat down to catch up.

But, in truth, the last thing she wanted to do was to be social, not when so much was at stake.

CHAPTER
FORTY-ONE

BEAR REALLY DID HAVE to grade some papers and turn them in. But there was also something else on his mind.

Ever since Piper had told him about the scandal surrounding her last official case with the Chicago PD, he hadn't been able to stop thinking about it.

And there was something he might be able to do to help her.

Part of being good with technology meant that he also knew how to get into computer systems that he wasn't supposed to get into.

He rubbed the back of his neck as he considered what he was about to do.

But if there was one thing he hated, it was when people were treated unjustly. And that seemed to be exactly what had happened to Piper.

If she could clear her name . . . then she could continue providing an excellent service to the police. Maybe even the FBI.

It meant that she might not want to stick around Fog Lake. But that wouldn't surprise him. He hadn't expected her to want to stay.

And even though he knew it was going to hurt when she left, the thing he wanted the most was for her to be happy.

If that meant he had to sacrifice his own happiness to see that then so be it.

After one more moment of hesitation, he dove into his project.

He'd sent Tim a phishing email yesterday.

He'd been sure Tim wouldn't take the bait.

But he had.

Bear's heart thrummed in his ears at the realization.

He didn't make it a habit to hack into other people's computers. It wasn't even legal. But, in this case, it seemed necessary.

Bear poked around for several minutes, exploring different folders and documents. When he saw two calculator apps, he knew he'd hit the jackpot.

One of the apps was often used as a cover to hide sensitive information. After a few tries, he figured out the code, and the files opened.

Pictures of Daniel Barr. By himself. And pictures of the victim. By himself.

Then an image of the two men together.

Photoshopped.

Not by Piper but by Tim.

Was Piper's theory correct? Had this guy set her up in order to get the promotion himself?

It was the only thing that made sense.

Bear stood, knowing he needed to share what he'd learned with Piper.

But before he headed downstairs his phone rang. It was his friend Rick. Bear had called him last week to ask about an event where Bear had been asked to present a lecture.

The two had gone to school together and still helped each other out on occasion—especially if either one had a question they needed to bounce off someone. Rick had been a great friend and went on Bear's annual ski trip with him.

Bear almost ignored the call but decided at the last minute to answer.

"Hey, Rick, what's going on?"

"I saw you on TV and remembered I never called you back. The event is great. I think you should do it."

"Thanks for the feedback. But . . . you said you saw me on TV?"

"That's right. Sounds like some crazy things are happening in your hometown."

One of those reporters must have filmed him going into the sheriff's office.

Bear glanced at the door, anxious to talk to Piper. He would need to keep this conversation short.

"Crazy is an understatement," Bear said. "This town has had more than its fair share of struggles."

"Sounds like it. Hey, I know it's kind of late, and I don't usually call. But there was something I just thought I would mention to you."

"What's that?"

"When I saw the video footage of you, I noticed Piper Stephens with you. Is she working the case?"

"Not exactly. She has a personal connection to it, however."

"I was involved in that case against Daniel Barr."

"Were you? I had no idea."

"And I just thought I'd try to be a good friend and let you know that you need to be careful around her."

"I know all about that altered photo."

"But there's something that wasn't exactly made public with that. A large cash amount showed up in a mystery bank account with Piper's name on it. People believe she was paid off to verify that photo."

Bear's heart beat harder.

Was his friend telling the truth? Could Piper have taken money in exchange for verifying the authenticity of a photograph? What if she was in on something with Tim? What if they both had something to gain from altering the photo?

Because if there was one thing Bear valued, it was integrity. He didn't expect perfection from people. But he also didn't like to be tricked.

He thanked his friend and ended the call.

But Rick had given Bear something to think about.

———

"Look at this!" Piper exclaimed as she pointed at her screen.

Luna leaned closer. "What am I looking at?"

"This guy sent out this blooper reel, for a lack of a better term. I'm sure he thought he was being clever. But he slipped up."

"What do you mean?" Luna squinted trying to get a better look.

Piper blew up the area she was looking at. "Right here in her glasses . . . you can see a reflection of a man. And he's not wearing a mask."

Luna sucked in a breath. "You're right. But it's hard to make out any of his features."

"I can run it through a couple of programs and see if I can clarify it. But if we can catch a glimpse of his reflection, then we might be able to figure out who this guy is. We could end this."

"End what?" a deep voice said.

Piper glanced over and saw Bear standing on the staircase. She quickly filled him in on what she had learned.

His eyes widened, and he came to take a look for himself. "This could be the break we've been waiting for. Good work."

Before they could talk about it anymore, his phone rang again. He shoved it to his ear and paced away from her. As his conversation went on, his voice became more urgent. When he disconnected and turned back to her, the aloofness Piper thought she'd seen in his eyes earlier was now unobstructed.

"Did you tell the media that Rebecca was another victim of The Good Samaritan Killer?"

Piper blinked in surprise. "No. Why would you ask that?"

"Because only a handful of people know. You just found out, and now the story has leaked. It's already running in some of the online magazines."

Her heart beat harder when she heard the accusation in his tone. "I wouldn't do that."

"What about the money that mysteriously showed up in your account after that trial?"

The air left her lungs.

"I think I'm going to turn in for the night." Luna rose and slipped away.

As she did, Piper stared at Bear, feeling like everything was falling apart.

————

Bear stared at Piper, waiting to hear her explanation.

Isaac had called to tell him that Rebecca was upset. Since Rebecca had just told Piper what had happened, they felt it prudent to call and see if she had been the one to inform the media.

"That money isn't what you think," Piper started.

"If it's not what I think then why didn't you tell me about it?"

"Because I know how it looks." Her chin trembled. "I know it looks like I took a bribe to somehow throw the investigation. But I didn't do that."

"Then where did that money come from?"

"I've been trying to figure that out. Somebody set up an account in my name and put the money there, knowing it would make me look guilty if push came to shove."

"But you need to sign paperwork to open bank

accounts. There are ways to prove someone forged your signature on the documents."

"It was all set up online. Someone digitally signed using my name, my birthdate. They even knew my social security number. But it wasn't me."

"And who do you think would do that?"

"The only person I've been able to think of is Tim. But I don't know why he would do something like that to me. He wanted the promotion, but that seems extreme even for him."

Bear thought about the information he'd dug up on Tim. Part of him wanted to share what he'd learned with Piper, but another part of him didn't know if he could trust her.

He *wanted* to believe he could.

But memories of Sasha's betrayal pummeled him and played on his insecurities.

Was Piper using him? Was she the type who'd do anything to get ahead? The type who'd compromise her integrity for the right amount of money?

Piper rose to her feet and took a step closer. But Bear raised his hand, warning her to stay back.

She stared at him, obvious strain in her gaze. "I didn't do this. I didn't talk to the media about Rebecca either. I promise I didn't."

"What about that phone call I overheard? The one

REFUGE OF REDEMPTION   291

where you promised someone you'd keep them updated?"

She froze before letting out a breath. "You heard that? My boss called and said I might be able to get my job back if I redeemed myself with this case. He said if I proved myself valuable to this investigation, it could help restore my reputation and I might be able to get my career back."

"I'm surprised you didn't mention that to me. It seems like something you would bring up."

"I thought about it, but there's just been so much going on. Besides that, I want to solve this case for Julie, not just so I can get my job back."

"So, are you going back to Chicago if they offer you the job?"

She shrugged and then shook her head before shrugging again. "I don't know. I don't really enjoy working with my boss. But I do enjoy forensic photography. I guess everything in my life kind of feels like a mess right now . . . everything but you."

Bear wanted to delight in her words, but he couldn't.

If Piper had hidden those things from him, then there was no telling what else she might be hiding. He wanted to trust her motivation, that it was true. But he'd been let down so many times before.

Was that what he was setting himself up for? More disappointment with Piper?

That's what his gut told him.

"Bear . . . please. I wouldn't just up and leave without talking to you about it first. I wouldn't take a bribe either. Or leak info to the press."

Tension still pulled across his chest. "I want to believe you but . . . I just don't know right now."

"Bear . . ."

"I've got to go to bed. Maybe we can talk more in the morning. Or maybe you should just look for somewhere else to stay starting tomorrow."

Piper gaped, almost as if she'd been slapped.

He didn't want to say the words. But he had to be realistic here. If he didn't trust Piper, he couldn't let her keep staying in his house anymore.

If she had really taken that bribe, she could ruin his reputation—the reputation he'd been trying to build in the years since his dad had been arrested.

If she had told him about the money upfront, and about the possibility of getting her job back . . . they may not be in this spot right now. But her secrets had served to drive a wedge between them.

Before Piper could say anything else, Bear offered a wave and headed back upstairs.

He needed some time to be by himself.

How could Bear think she would have done those things?

He didn't really know her at all, did he?

Piper sank into the couch and buried her face in her hands.

Just when she felt hopeful that circumstances might be getting better, this had happened. The one person who had seemed to really believe in her now thought she was untrustworthy.

Maybe she couldn't blame Bear. Maybe she should have told him about that money.

But she knew how it would look even though she hadn't touched a dime of it. Instead, she'd immediately reported it to her supervisor, and his team had been trying to track down the origin of the account ever since.

Probably more to prove her guilt than her innocence.

But she was trying to trust the system—even if that very system had fired her.

For a while, she'd let herself imagine what it might be like to move to Fog Lake. To do her forensic photography and image analysis on the side. Maybe to teach some classes and do more guest lectures. But to settle in for a simpler life.

Maybe even a life with Bear.

She could have seen them being happy together for a long time.

But all that seemed impossible now.

An ache filled her chest until a tear trickled down her cheek.

Her friend Julie was out there. Piper had no right to feel heartbroken right now, not considering what Julie was going through.

Yet she couldn't stop the emotions from flowing through her.

Bear was right. In the morning, she needed to leave. She'd overstayed her welcome. And now Piper needed to figure out what her future was going to look like.

CHAPTER
FORTY-TWO

IT'S time to put my plan into action.

And I know exactly how everything will play out.

I smile as I grab my night vision goggles.

Piper won't be able to turn down my proposition.

And it's now become essential that I stop her.

She is getting too close to the truth.

I can't let her expose me.

Anger begins to singe my blood, but I hold it back. I need to save that energy for later.

I leave my house, but I don't get in my car. I can hike where I need to go. That fact has served me well over the past several weeks.

I hope Piper believes that old mine is safe.

Because my plans for her are a doozy.

The mine is going to end up being her grave.

I'm a genius.

I smile again.

I also have other ideas.

Brilliant ideas.

Ideas that will be my crowning glory.

Everyone will fear me.

They will know I'm not stupid or incompetent.

That I'm the one in control.

I can't wait anymore to get started.

CHAPTER
FORTY-THREE

PIPER AWOKE WITH A START.

She jerked her eyes open and flung herself up in bed.

Darkness surrounded her.

Darkness and quiet.

Except for the person in the room with her.

She blinked a few times, trying to get things to come into focus.

Luna?

Her intern stared at her from the edge of the bed, a frown on her face. "I'm sorry to wake you. I didn't know what to do. But then I decided to let you be the judge of it. This needs to be your decision."

"What are you talking about?" Piper ran a hand through her hair as they talked in hushed tones.

"I just got a tip on the website I set up. It was addressed to you."

Suddenly, her grogginess disappeared. "What did it say?"

"I got a video for you saying that you should go to the mine alone tonight. That you could be traded for Julie. That this is your only chance to save your friend. Otherwise, she'll die."

"What?" Piper's voice sounded breathless as she tried to comprehend what was being said.

Luna held up her phone, clicked on a few buttons, and then thrust it in Piper's face. "It's here."

Piper blinked a few more times as the screen came into focus.

It was Julie.

She spoke to the camera, tears in her gaze. "He says I'll die if you don't come. He wants to meet you in the mine by the main entrance so we can do a tradeoff. Your life for mine. And you have to come alone . . . or . . . or he'll kill me!" Her voice cracked as her face twisted with terror. "Don't do it, Piper—"

Before she could finish, the video cut off.

Piper's heart pounded in her ears.

This guy was giving her a chance to save Julie.

As Piper remembered Julie's grieving parents, she knew she didn't have much choice.

This was all her doing. If Piper hadn't asked her

assistant to go into that mine with her, Julie would be safe at home right now.

"What are you going to do?" Luna stared at her with wide, fearful eyes.

Piper flung herself out of bed. "I've got to go. I've got to meet him."

Luna grasped her arm. "Piper . . . are you sure that's a good idea? He could just kill you both."

"It's a chance I have to take. I won't be able to live with myself if I don't try."

"Should you tell the FBI? Bear?"

"Julie said if I don't come alone that he'll kill her. I can't take that chance."

"What am I supposed to do?" Luna's voice cracked. "Let me come with you."

Piper pulled her shoes on. "Then you'll just get killed also. I can't let that happen. But I *would* like for you to wait a couple of hours and then tell Bear. By that time, the exchange should be done. Someone will need to go and get Julie."

"Piper . . ." Moisture glistened in Luna's eyes.

Piper threw her arms around Luna when she saw the despair in the girl's eyes. "It's going to be okay."

Luna shook her head. "No, it's not."

Piper licked her lips, wanting to dispute the statement. But she couldn't. Because she had a feeling this wasn't going to have a happy ending for her.

But she had to do everything she could to help her friend.

Even if it meant putting her own life on the line.

————

Bear heard a sound and sat up in bed. He reached for the gun that he always kept in the nightstand beside him.

Was someone in his house? Someone besides Piper and Luna?

They should both be asleep right now.

His heart pounded in his ears as he paused to listen.

And he heard it. A creak. Almost like a door was opening and closing.

Quickly, he got out of bed and threw some clothes on. Holding his gun, he crept into the hallway.

But everything was silent again.

Then he heard tires on gravel.

Was someone coming to his house?

No, he realized. Someone was leaving.

He rushed downstairs to the front door just in time to see taillights disappearing down the driveway.

In the darkness, he couldn't tell whose car it was.

Instead, he rushed back upstairs and knocked on Piper's door.

There was no answer.

"Piper?" He twisted the knob and opened her door, hoping he'd see that she was still in bed safe and sound.

"She's gone," someone said behind him.

He quickly turned around and saw Luna standing outside the other spare bedroom. "What do you mean she's gone?"

Luna rubbed her throat as her tumultuous gaze met his. "Piper told me not to tell you. Not yet."

"Did she leave . . . because of our fight?" Bear had instantly regretted his words last night. Was it too late to take them back?

"She . . . she has to help Julie."

Bear stepped closer, questions pounding in his ears. "What do you mean help Julie?"

Luna pressed her lips together, clearly hesitant to share any more details.

"You have to tell me what's going on, Luna," Bear said. "Especially if Piper could be in danger."

"She told me not to."

"Luna . . . I know you care about Piper. And if she's about to do something that she could regret then I need to help her."

Luna stared at him another moment before

nodding. She pulled something up on her phone and showed him.

Bear felt the blood drain from his face as he watched the video.

"Tell me she didn't go to meet this guy to trade herself for Julie?"

But when Luna didn't respond, he knew the answer.

He had to go after her.

Because if Piper went into that mine alone, then Bear knew there was a good chance he would never see her again.

CHAPTER
FORTY-FOUR

PIPER'S LIMBS TREMBLED UNCONTROLLABLY.

She knew this was a bad idea, but she didn't know what else to do. She felt certain this monster would make good on his threat. If she showed up with anyone else, he would simply kill Julie.

But that didn't stop her fear as Piper pulled over to the side of the road, cut her engine, and climbed out.

This hike had been difficult in the daytime with other people along. But hiking through the woods alone in the dark?

The idea had trouble written all over it.

But she'd come this far. She needed to keep going.

Piper had messed up so many times already. She didn't want another regret to add to her list.

With that in mind, she grabbed her flashlight and started up the trail. She didn't have any time to waste. It had taken her an hour and a half to make it to the mine last time. But she didn't think she had that kind of time tonight. She needed to move as quickly as possible.

The woods around her seemed eerily quiet. It was almost like there were animals out there who knew she shouldn't be here. Animals that were watching her.

But were they prey or were they hunters?

She shivered again, and her lungs tightened.

Bear's image came to her mind.

Piper desperately wished that she had had the chance to make things right with him. To explain herself. To somehow make him believe her.

But there was no time for that. Maybe, as more time went by, he would discover the truth. He would realize that Piper had always tried to act on the side of the law, that she wouldn't purposefully verify a photo that wasn't real.

She continued climbing, her feet slipping on the slicker rocks. She remembered what it was like hiking that day with Bear when he'd helped her through the difficult parts of the path. When he'd caught her when she had almost fallen into the icy water.

Then she remembered maneuvering behind that waterfall and kissing Bear.

The moment had been like something out of her dreams.

But apparently, dreams weren't meant to last forever.

She swallowed back the thoughts and continued up the mountainside.

The only comfort she took in the situation was in the hope that Julie might survive this.

————

Bear hurried down the road. He had to catch Piper before she did something she regretted. He knew she was probably trying to be noble. But this was no time to try to be a hero. There was no way she could trust this guy or believe that he would do what he said.

This killer had simply wanted to lure her out.

After the emotional battering Bear had given Piper last night, she probably hadn't been thinking clearly. Otherwise, she would have never gone alone.

Bear had already called Shane, and he and his guys were also on their way. Piper might hate him for interrupting her plan. But he couldn't live with himself if he simply let her go to this mine where she would certainly die.

He pulled to the side of the road and parked behind her car.

Bear had probably left only ten minutes behind her. He'd taken enough time to pull on some hiking boots, to grab his backpack, gun, and flashlight, and then leave. And he knew that he was a faster hiker than she was.

He would catch up with Piper in time.

There was no other acceptable outcome.

Pulling on his backpack, he gripped his flashlight and started up the trail.

He imagined Piper walking up this way by herself. It wasn't smart. Hiking alone at night? Never a good idea.

Add a serial killer into the mix, and it could turn deadly. Fast.

As Bear maneuvered up the mountain all he could do was pray. Pray that he reached her in time and that nothing happened to her.

Because despite the tension between them, he cared about her. And the last thing he wanted was for her to be hurt.

CHAPTER
FORTY-FIVE

PIPER FINALLY REACHED the top of the incline and sucked in ragged gulps of air. She really needed to up her cardiovascular game—if she survived.

But she had only a moment to try to catch her breath. In the distance she saw the train tracks that led to the old mine.

This was it.

The moment she would find out how this would play out.

The moment she would find out if this guy would let Julie go.

When she would discover what this guy planned to do with her.

She didn't really want to know. She wished she

would wake up and discover this was all a nightmare.

But she knew it wasn't.

Piper straightened her back and drew in a deep breath. Then she started toward the mine entrance.

As she walked, she didn't see any other signs of life.

It was like she was the only person up here.

But she felt certain that the Understudy was nearby.

That he was watching.

That he was simply waiting to make his move.

With a touch of hesitation, she slipped through the gate and into the tunnel leading deep into the heart of the mountain.

Shivers overwhelmed her as she took several more steps into the darkness.

Her lungs were so tight she could hardly breathe.

"Hello?" she called.

She stared in front of her at the two tunnels where they split.

The one where those bodies had been found.

This guy was sick.

What was he planning?

She wouldn't put anything past him.

She wanted to run. To get out of here.

She took a step back, her instincts telling her to flee.

But before she could, she heard a footstep behind her.

Then a pungent spray hit her face, and everything went black.

———

Just as Bear crested the top of the incline and glanced at the North Elk Ridge Mine, he saw a light flicker off.

Was that Piper?

He picked up his pace as he darted toward the entrance.

"Piper!" he called.

He didn't care if anyone else heard. In fact, he wanted this guy to hear that he was here. He wanted to scare him away.

Bear heard footsteps running in the mine.

He shone his light around, trying to figure out the direction the sound had come from.

Was that Piper running away? Or the killer?

Bear went several more feet into the east tunnel when the beam of his flashlight caught something.

Someone lying on the ground.

"Piper . . ."

Quickly, he darted toward her. She appeared unconscious.

He shook her, patting her cheeks. "Piper? Can you hear me?"

She moaned before opening her eyes.

She blinked several times before pushing herself up. "Where is he?"

Bear gripped his flashlight and shone it in the distance, looking for the man who'd done this to her.

But all he saw was darkness.

"He must have run away," Bear told her.

"He was just right here. He was wearing those night vision goggles so he could see. You must have scared him away. But Julie . . ."

"I doubt he brought Julie with him," Bear told her. "You should have told me you were coming."

A knot formed between her eyes, and she glanced away. "You weren't exactly talking to me."

"Maybe we can save that discussion for another time. We need to get out of here."

He helped her to her feet and gave her a moment to steady herself. But just as they started walking toward the mine entrance, an explosion filled the air.

Bear grabbed Piper and pulled her back, shielding her with his body as dust billowed from the avalanche of rocks and debris.

When it was over, Bear glanced toward the opening and shined his light on the rubble.

Their exit appeared to be totally blocked.

CHAPTER
FORTY-SIX

PIPER FELT tears press her eyes.

They were trapped in this tunnel. And even though she knew there were other ways to get out, it would be challenging to find them.

It was so dark. So cold.

And a killer lurked in here with them. A killer who could see them. Hunt them.

"It's going to be okay." Bear's voice sounded confident. "We'll find a way out of here."

"But what about what Rex said about the dangers of gases in the mines? Or how the floor can suddenly drop out into a deep shaft? Or what if it starts raining and floods, and the tunnels fill with water, and we're trapped—"

"I know that there are risks." Bear's firm voice cut through her fear. "But we're going to do whatever we can to get out of here. Plus, it's not supposed to rain. You put together that map showing the other entrances and exits. Do you remember which one was closest to this tunnel entrance?"

Piper searched her thoughts, trying to figure out what the closest shaft entrance would be. But her mind felt too scrambled. She couldn't remember.

"Maybe we should just try to dig out," she said.

Bear shined his light back toward the entrance. "This guy wanted to trap you in here. He set up some type of explosive to make that happen. If I had to guess, this rubble is a few feet thick and probably not very stable. If we start trying to dig out, we could cause more of this tunnel to collapse."

She shuddered. He was right. But any way she looked at it, this situation was risky.

Just as the thought went through her mind, the tunnel moaned around them as if threatening to collapse even more.

Bear grabbed her hand. "Come on. Let's check out what's farther down here."

Piper didn't really want to. She didn't want to move, out of fear of the unknown. Yet at the same time she had little choice. What if this guy had planted more explosives?

Their best bet was to move, just like Bear said.

But that didn't stop the terror from coursing through her.

————

Bear knew the direness of the situation, but he didn't want to reiterate it for Piper. She was already scared enough as it was.

Finding a way out of these tunnels was going to be challenging. Plus, the explosion could have compromised the structure of the beams holding these tunnels in place.

But the best thing he could do right now was to stay positive but realistic.

Making the whole situation worse was the fact that this killer could still be hiding somewhere in here, just waiting to strike.

One of the only things that brought Bear comfort was the fact that he'd called the FBI. Hopefully, they would arrive on the scene soon. They would realize that Bear and Piper were trapped in this tunnel.

Would they try to dig them out?

It was a possibility.

Or they could also use another entrance into the mine.

Right now, sitting around not doing anything wasn't an option.

Bear kept Piper close, their argument from last night temporarily forgotten. All that mattered at the moment was surviving.

"You shouldn't have come here alone," Bear finally muttered.

Piper sent him a dirty look. "Are you really going to lecture me right now?"

"Piper . . . if I hadn't shown up . . ." Emotion clogged his throat.

"Then maybe Julie would be free."

"You really think this guy brought Julie with him?" His voice rose with emotion. "Did you see her? Did she call out to you?"

"Maybe he put tape over her mouth." But Piper's clipped tone seemed to indicate she didn't believe that theory either.

"Come on, Piper. You had to know she wasn't here. That was never his plan."

Her shoulders remained tight as she shrugged. "I didn't know anything—only that I had to do whatever I could to help."

"And that's what this guy was banking on." Anger coursed through Bear at the thought. This killer had preyed on Piper's kindness—and on her guilt—to put her in this situation.

They continued down the tunnel, which became more and more narrow as they went. They moved slowly. Hurrying through something like this could lead to a misstep they couldn't recover from.

"I don't want to argue," Piper said. "I know I've made a lot of mistakes. Everyone knows that. But at the end of the day, I'm just trying to do my best."

His heart panged with a moment of compassion when he heard the sincerity in her voice.

He paused as they reached another Y in the tunnel. He drew in a breath as he contemplated which direction they should go. There were all kinds of dangers in here. Including the gases that could oxidize. Plus, he wasn't sure about the oxygen levels in this space.

"Which way do you think we should go?" Piper frantically glanced between the tunnels.

"To the right. If we go to the left, we'll just be going deeper into the center of the mountain. Our chances are better if we go to the right. If it was daylight outside, we could look for little rays of illumination creeping in through openings. But it's going to be more challenging since it's dark."

He felt the tremble rake through her, but she nodded, and they kept walking. As the ceiling became lower, he hunched down. He hoped the space didn't get much smaller than this. Because he could sense the panic starting to set in for Piper.

Sweat beaded on her brow. She started to shake.

Her breathing became shallow. And she'd grown quiet.

None of which were good signs.

As he took another step forward, he paused. He squeezed Piper's hand, urging her to stop.

"What is it?" she whispered.

He didn't want to make things worse for her, but he had to tell her the truth. "I think someone is in here with us."

CHAPTER
FORTY-SEVEN

PIPER COULD HARDLY BREATHE.

Her heart pounded in her ears so loudly she couldn't hear much else.

Sweat covered her skin, and instinct warned her of danger.

The killer was watching them right now, wasn't he? What else did he have planned?

She and Bear froze, but even as they did, she knew that this guy wore night vision goggles. He could probably see everything they were doing right now. He could have a gun, and they wouldn't even see it. They wouldn't even know what was coming.

Another shiver wracked her body.

What could they do? Just standing here didn't seem smart. But she didn't want to walk toward danger either.

"Bear?" Piper's voice came out just below a whisper, hardly audible even to her own ears.

"Do you feel that?"

"Feel what?"

"It's a breeze. We must be close to an entrance."

Hope surged through her.

Just as his words settled in her ears, she heard another footstep.

But not one that had been made in secret.

Piper heard footsteps pounding in the distance. Maybe even outside this cave.

She gripped Bear's hand harder as she tried to anticipate what might happen next.

She didn't have to wait long. A light shone down from above. Three shadowed men loomed overhead.

"Bear? Piper?"

She'd recognize that voice anywhere.

Special Agent Townsend.

He had found them.

Now she just prayed they could get out of here and back to safety in one piece.

————

Twenty minutes later, Bear and Piper leaned against an ORV with blankets around them. They had been successfully rescued from the mine—thank goodness.

Piper had gone through the story of why she had come out, and Bear listened.

He was glad he'd shown up when he did.

If he'd arrived just a few minutes later, Piper might not be here right now.

Bear could say the same for the FBI and the team they'd brought with them. Their appearance happened at just the right time. Even though he suspected the killer was still somewhere in that tunnel, Bear knew that when the authorities had arrived, the guy would have fled.

"How about if I have someone take you two back to your truck, Bear?" Shane stood in front of them.

Bear nodded. "That sounds like a good plan."

A park ranger loaded them into an off-road vehicle and took them down the mountain to Bear's truck. They'd come to pick up Piper's car later. She was in no state to drive.

Piper and Bear silently road back to his place.

As soon as they walked into Bear's house, Luna rushed toward them.

"You're okay!" She threw her arms around Piper. "Where's Julie?"

Piper shook her head. "She wasn't there."

Luna's face fell. "I'm sorry. I had high hopes."

Piper nodded and shoved a hair behind her ear. "I know. Me too. I hate that she's still missing. But for now, I think I'm going to take a shower and see if I can get cleaned up." She glanced back at Bear. "Then I'll pack my things. As soon as I can get my car back . . ."

"You don't have to leave," Bear said, his voice sounding hoarse.

"I think it would be for the best. If you'll just give me a couple hours and let me figure out how to get my car . . ."

"I can give you a ride," Luna offered. "I'll need to leave too."

Piper nodded, but something close to agony stained her gaze. "That sounds great."

As she slipped up the stairs, regret filled him.

Bear needed to talk to her before she left. Needed to clear the air.

Because he wasn't sure what exactly had happened with the case she had worked. But she did deserve to have someone listen to her side of the story. Of the whole story.

CHAPTER
FORTY-EIGHT

WHEN PIPER LEFT Bear's place, she knew she wouldn't be able to go back to Lexington. There was too much to do here still.

She didn't have much money, but she would use what she had to get a hotel room. She would keep looking for Julie with or without Bear's help.

As much as she wanted to be angry and upset with Bear, she couldn't be. He *had* saved her tonight. Besides, she knew how the situation back in Chicago looked. She'd only hoped he'd give her the benefit of the doubt.

But life didn't always work that way.

After her shower, she dressed and sat on her bed, waiting for her hair to dry some. She would wait until it was daylight before she went to get her car, just for safety reasons. Plus, she needed to get some sleep.

Not that she was tired right now.

Out of curiosity, she grabbed her computer and opened it to do a quick search. As she did, photos she'd loaded from her camera popped onto the screen.

One of them was of Bear.

She paused to study it a moment.

She'd taken the picture of him when they were hiking to that mineshaft. Brittle trees stretched in the background along with stately rocks. The sun captured his features, making his green eyes gleam. Shadows hit his chest at just the right angle to show his broad shoulders and tapered waist.

He was so handsome.

She couldn't help but think the two of them could have had something beautiful together.

Except he was just like everyone else.

He didn't believe her.

He thought Piper was doing whatever necessary to get ahead—including taking bribes.

An ache filled her chest.

That realization hurt more than she wanted to admit.

She quickly clicked off the photo and did a Google search. She'd wanted to do some more research on OJ and OD. She still felt like the two men could offer some valuable information on the Understudy.

After all, there had to be a reason the killer had chosen to hide the bodies in the tunnel there. She knew OJ was probably in his eighties, and she had no idea if he was alive or what his health might be. Since OD was younger, he seemed like a better person to talk to.

She typed in "North Elk Ridge Mine + OD," but no results came up.

Piper paused and nibbled on her bottom lip for a moment as she thought about another way to search.

Was OD short for something?

She tried a few more combinations until she finally got the results that she was looking for.

She sucked in a breath.

OD was actually Dell, Bear's neighbor. Full name: Odell Tatum. He and his brother must have different fathers since they also had different last names.

Piper shook her head, unsure if she was understanding this correctly.

She typed in Odell Tatum and watched as the results populated the screen.

A picture of Bear's neighbor appeared.

He was *definitely* the same man.

And he went by OD.

Her heart pounded harder.

She did another search and discovered that, after OD had left the mining industry, he'd received a small payout. He got a job working as a supervisor with waste management in Sevierville.

Piper kept searching for more information.

Another article detailed how he took the money he'd made from the mines and invested it in another company.

A company that was developing innovative trail cams.

He was selling proprietary footage from trail cams to potential hunters . . .

Disgust churned in her gut.

Had the guy they'd been looking for been right in front of them this whole time?

She snapped her computer shut and stood.

She needed to run this by someone else.

Bear.

Because she couldn't be sure . . . but the fact that this guy lived close to Bear, that he was connected with the mines, and that he'd invested in a trail cam developer . . .

Could he be the person that they were looking for?

She rushed down the stairs, but as soon as she hit

the bottom step, she heard voices coming from the kitchen.

As she rounded the corner, she saw that Bear's family was here . . . along with a man she had never seen before.

Was that . . . ?

Piper shook her head. No, it couldn't be.

————

Bear looked up from his cup of coffee and saw Piper standing there, obvious surprise on her face.

He stepped toward her, hating the uneasiness jostling inside him. "Piper, this is my father, James Colson. Dad, this is Piper. Isaac just picked Dad up, and he's now officially a free man."

Piper's eyebrows shot up. She shook her head, seeming to pull herself together, before extending her hand. "Mr. Colson, it's so nice to meet you. I'm glad that the justice system is finally making things right."

"It's good to be here. I've waited a long time for this day." His dad shook Piper's hand, an earnest look in his eyes.

Bear hadn't expected his father to be here right now. But Isaac had called about an hour ago and said he was on his way.

Bear had quickly thrown together a breakfast,

wanting to do something to make his father feel welcome. Meanwhile, Madison had shown up as well as Rebecca. Shane would have joined them, but he was busy investigating the case.

While all of this happened, Luna hung back on the couch, working quietly on her computer and giving the family space.

Bear glanced at Piper and thought he saw a certain urgency in her eyes.

Had she learned something new in the brief amount of time she'd been in her room?

The two of them could talk again in a moment.

Right now, he didn't want anything to put a damper on this reunion.

Today was what he and his siblings had hoped and prayed about for so long now.

His dad glanced around the room, emotion welling in his gaze. "I can't believe we're finally all back together. I wasn't sure this day would ever happen."

"That's mostly thanks to Isaac," Bear said. "He's been working hard to have you freed."

"Bear's being modest," Isaac said. "We've all really had to work together over these past several months. What's been happening here in Fog Lake has been a tragedy. But the good thing that's come out of it is that these new crimes revealed the truth—that you're not guilty."

His father ran a hand beneath his eyes as moisture pooled there. "And I'm thankful for that. I'm just sorry that more people had to get hurt in the process."

"We all are." Madison squeezed her Dad's arm. "Now, if the FBI can just catch this other guy, maybe we can all finally move on from this."

Bear liked that idea.

But there was still so much unresolved.

As he looked at Rebecca, he saw her glancing at Piper. Rebecca wasn't sure that she could trust Piper, was she? And Bear couldn't blame her after everything that had happened.

But now that some of his emotions had worn off, he wished he'd heard Piper's side of the story before jumping to conclusions.

He hoped she'd have a chance to share it with him. He wanted to know about the look in her eyes right now also. Had she discovered something new?

Bear pulled some muffins out of the oven as Isaac fried eggs on the griddle.

They would all sit down and have a nice meal together. Just for a moment they would be a complete family.

After that, reality would kick in again. This whole

process wasn't going to be as easy as some people might romanticize. Certainly, his father had changed in those years in prison. Plus, he hadn't been the man Bear thought he was anyway. They would all need to get to know Dad again, while sorting through everything that had happened. And Bear was going to need to talk to Piper . . . and hopefully clear the air.

CHAPTER
FORTY-NINE

PIPER STARED AT JAMES COLSON. She couldn't believe he was here. That he had been released from prison.

Bear and his brother and sister had to be thrilled.

When she remembered the news she needed to share, another round of guilt filled her. Piper needed to tell them what she'd learned. But she hated to break up this happy reunion.

Maybe she could give them a few moments of peace before she broke the news . . .

Her throat tightened as she crept closer to the breakfast bar, trying to look more at ease than she actually felt.

She shouldn't be here, shouldn't be intruding on this moment with them. Which was a shame because in the brief time she'd been around these people, they'd felt like family. That wasn't something Piper could say about very many people.

It seemed as if just when happiness had been dangled in front of her, it was snatched away again. Maybe this was her lot in life.

Piper's gaze caught Rebecca's. Piper wanted to explain to Rebecca that she hadn't been the one to share the news about what had happened to her. But it would be awkward to bring it up now in front of everyone.

"Let me get you some coffee." Rebecca smiled and rose from her seat.

That was unexpected. Had something changed? Had Rebecca simply decided to forgive her without even hearing any defense or explanation?

Based on the gentle look in Rebecca's eyes, it didn't appear Rebecca blamed her or had any animosity toward Piper.

Piper hoped her gut feeling was correct.

"Thank you," she managed to croak out.

Piper wished she could be that quick to forgive herself. But she'd been self-loathing ever since Julie disappeared.

She lingered on the fringe, listening as the Colsons caught up and chatted.

For a moment, the scene felt so normal. So happy. Almost as if all the bad things hadn't happened.

As Julie's image filled her mind again, Piper knew she couldn't stay quiet anymore. Every second counted right now.

She needed to share what she'd learned, even if it broke up the joy in the air.

Piper cleared her throat, trying to find the right words. Trying to find a good break in the conversation.

Before she could do that, a knock sounded at the door.

She glanced around.

All the Colsons were here. Was it Townsend?

And, if so, why hadn't they heard his car pulling up?

Bear strode toward the door and jerked it open.

The person Piper saw standing on the other side made her blood grow cold.

———

"Dell," Bear muttered as he stared at his neighbor. "What brings you by?"

Bear stepped back and extended his arm, inviting his neighbor out of the cold.

Dell stepped inside and tugged at his coat before turning toward everyone. "I'm sorry to stop by uninvited. It looks like you have something going on."

Bear glanced back at his family. "I have a minute. What's up?"

"After we talked the other day, I thought I should let you know that I saw someone creeping around your house this morning."

Alarm shot through Bear. "What?"

"I was walking around the woods. When I got to the edge of my property line, I could barely see your house. I wasn't trying to spy on you. But I saw someone in black walking out by your garage. Maybe it was one of your family members. I can't be sure."

No one in Bear's family was wearing all black. "Good to know."

"Anyway, since you seemed curious about anyone being on your property, I thought I should let you know. I would have called, but my cell phone isn't working."

"I appreciate that. I'll check that out." What would someone have been doing on his property? Bear hadn't seen any signs of anything wrong when he had gone out this morning to feed the chickens.

But that didn't mean that someone hadn't been there.

He glanced back at Piper, wondering what she was thinking about all this.

Her face had gone pale, and she opened her

mouth as if she wanted to say something, but no words came out.

Why was she reacting like this?

"Piper?" He stared at her, determined to get to the bottom of what was going on.

She touched her throat as she took a step back, as if afraid.

Then she pointed at Dell. "He . . . he's the killer."

CHAPTER
FIFTY

PIPER SAW the doubt on Bear's face. She couldn't
blame him.

As soon as she'd said the words, everybody in the
house had gone quiet and stared at her, waiting to
hear what she'd say next.

Before she could, Dell spoke. "Excuse me?"

She was done playing this game. She wasn't
going to let this guy plant any doubt in her mind.

This was the man they'd been looking for. He'd
truly been right in front of them the whole time.

"What are you talking about, Piper?" Bear stared
at her, his shoulders seeming to broaden as he stood
there facing Dell.

Piper didn't dare take her eyes off Dell. She didn't
trust him. Didn't know what he might be planning.

Had he seen someone on Bear's property? Or was that just meant as a distraction? A reason to come over and knock on Bear's door.

Was this just another part of the game he was playing with them?

"He goes by OD," Piper explained. "His half-brother owned the mine. OD worked there until they closed down. He moved away for a while—but not far away—and just recently bought the property next to Bear's."

"That's interesting, but that doesn't mean he's a killer." Doubt tinged Isaac's voice.

James Colson stepped closer, standing between Dell and Piper, his eyebrows pushed together as he listened intently. His hands went to his hips, and he looked ready to act if necessary.

"But what you don't know is that since the mine closed down, he has been using the money he made from it to invest in a new company that works with trail cams," Piper continued. "They're developing proprietary technology that will allow hunters to monitor various cams in certain areas so they can up their hunting game."

Bear glanced back at Dell. "Is that correct?"

"She's correct. But I'm still unsure how that makes me a killer." Dell let out a laugh. "This whole conversation seems a bit ridiculous, doesn't it?"

"We should have known," Piper continued. "Even the name of his hunting cabin? Deertail Hollow? His brother's last name was Deerman. It's almost like it was put there as a clue. And Dell could access that tunnel here on your property. He just bought his place six months ago. That's the perfect location to keep an eye on your family."

"This is compelling." Bear stared at her, questions in his gaze. "But that doesn't mean he's a killer."

"OD . . ." James Colson observed the man, his eyes steely.

"James . . ." Dell nodded slowly. "It's been a long time, hasn't it?"

That was right. Dell had said the two of them knew each other way back when. So, Dell could have known certain things about Mr. Colson, things that he could have used in order to plant clues.

"Listen." Dell took a step back, his motions suddenly stiff. "I didn't come here to start trouble. I just wanted to tell you what I saw. I can see now that was a mistake."

He took another step toward the door.

Was he going to leave? Without incident? Should they even let him?

Piper didn't know the answer to those questions.

But if this guy had grabbed Julie . . . then he

needed to be brought in for questioning before it was too late.

———

Bear's mind raced as he tried to sort through everything he'd just learned.

Piper's words made sense.

This man had been right in front of them the whole time. He had a bird's eye view of Bear's property. In fact, he even walked here so Bear hadn't heard anyone approaching.

Plus, there was the connection with the mine, with the trail cams, and with Bear's father.

The mining company had been prominent in the town for a long time, which probably meant that Ralph Burgess had some connections with the people running it. That was usually how politics and business worked. Was that how the two men knew each other?

"Wait, you don't believe her, do you?" Dell stared at him, something close to offense in his gaze.

"I think what she said has some validity that we should examine," Bear said.

"No offense, but isn't she the one who accepted money to verify a forged photo?"

Piper gasped. "How did you know about that? It was never made public."

"I have my ways of finding out these things." Satisfaction glistened in his gaze. "And I like to know who's around me. I do my research."

Bear liked this conversation less and less all the time. He grabbed his phone from his pocket. "I'm calling Special Agent Townsend so he can come over and clear the air."

"You don't want to do that." Dell shook his head, still looking unassuming.

Irritation pinched Bear's back muscles. "As a matter of fact, I do."

Dell raised his hand. "Before you do that, I just want you to take a moment and see if anything seems odd in this house right now."

Bear froze. "What do you mean?"

"Take a deep breath."

Against his better instincts, Bear obeyed.

What was that scent? Was it . . . gasoline?

Suddenly, Dell's eyes lit with excitement. In the blink of an eye, he reached into his pocket and withdrew a gun. "No one move. I *will* pull this trigger."

"If that gasoline is as strong as I think it is, then this whole place will go up in flames." Bear said. "With you inside also."

"It doesn't matter anymore. This is my *piece de resistance*. The Colsons have been integral in these crimes from the start. It only makes sense that you all go out in style."

Bear's father stepped closer, veins bulging at his neck as his muscles hardened. "What do you think you're doing?"

Dell shoved his gun forward. "Don't even think about it. Stay where you are, or I'll pull this trigger. I promise you I will."

Bear's thoughts raced. Even though Dell was outnumbered, he had a gun, and they didn't. Too bad he'd left his in his bedroom.

"You," Dell muttered looking at Luna. "I need you to get up. Take that basket on the floor. Collect everybody's cell phones. And if anyone has a gun on them—which I'm guessing no one does since you're here celebrating—I'll need those too. Don't try anything."

Something close to a growl started deep inside Bear.

He knew exactly what this guy was thinking.

Dell was going to stage this like a house fire he'd rushed into to try to save the people inside.

He would record everything.

Record how the Colsons all tragically died.

But this wasn't the way things were going to play out.

Just as the thought entered Bear's head, Dell shifted.

As he did, Bear saw a camera strapped to the man's chest just beneath his coat.

FIFTY-ONE

PIPER'S EYES widened when she saw the gun. When she heard the malice in Dell's voice. When she smelled the faint scent of gasoline in the air.

This man was crazy enough to try to kill all of them.

She had no doubt about that.

Certainly, there had to be something they could do.

Piper's stomach squeezed as she took her phone from her pocket and put it in the basket Luna held in front of her.

Poor Luna . . . why did she have to be here for this? Why did someone else have to suffer because of Piper's mistakes?

No, Piper told herself. This wasn't *her* mistake.

The only one responsible for what this man had done was Dell.

But, still, she wished her intern was somewhere safe instead of being here with them right now. Too many innocent people had already been hurt.

"Now, all of you," Dell muttered. "Go into the living room. Don't try anything. Don't test me."

Isaac raised his hands in the air, his voice calm. "You don't have to do this."

"Yes, I do. I've been planning this for years—the moment when all of you would be together again. It's like a dream come true."

"There are a lot of innocent people in this room," Bear said. "They don't need to suffer."

"No one has ever needed to suffer." Dell's voice rose with agitation. "That's never been the point. The point is showing you that I am powerful. No matter what my brother ever told me. Did you know he told me I'd never amount to anything?"

"I'm sorry that happened." James stepped closer. "But if your beef is with me then let everyone else go."

"You think I only have a problem with you?" Dell let out a harsh chuckle. "All I know is that Ralph hated you. That's enough for me. I knew you all would be perfect for my *piece de resistance*."

"Your *piece de resistance*?" Bear repeated, a knot forming between his eyes.

Piper didn't like the sound of that.

"What are you planning on doing with us?" Madison asked. "Why did you wait until we were all together?"

He smirked. "To show you all what I can do. I can't tell you how happy this moment makes me. It's going to be even better than I ever envisioned."

"How did you get involved with Burgess?" Isaac asked. "At least tell us that. Give us some answers."

Piper glanced at him. Certainly, Isaac was trying to buy time. To figure out a game plan here.

Piper tried to come up with an idea on how to get everyone safely out of here, but nothing came to mind. Even if she were to grab a makeshift weapon, by the time she reached Dell, he would pull the trigger.

Clearly, Bear was stronger than Dell. But that didn't matter when the man had a gun.

"Years ago, I caught Ralph killing Karen Davies, his second victim," Dell explained. "He thought I was going to turn him in. But, instead, I told him I wanted to help. I wanted to learn his ways. So, we set up an account on the dark web, and that's how we communicated. No one knew. All these years, that's what we've done."

"Are you the one who was the tech genius in all this?" Bear asked.

As the question filled the air, Piper's mind raced. Dell didn't seem like a tech genius. Sure, he'd invested in a company that focused on trail cams, but that didn't mean he was an expert.

So how had he figured out the videos? The security system?

"I'm going to have to lock you all in here now." Dell stepped back toward the door. "Don't try to get out any of the windows. I nailed them shut. I blocked the back door as well. But have no fear. I'll catch all the pandemonium on video, and millions will enjoy seeing the horrific moment when you think you're rescued but you're not."

Bear let out a growl and stepped closer. "You don't want to do that."

"Watch me." Before anyone could say anything else, Dell pulled the trigger. The next moment, James grabbed his shoulder.

He'd been hit.

Madison rushed to him, horror on her face.

"Why'd you do that?" Bear demanded.

"Because you guys need to know that I'm serious." Dell swept his gun across the room. "Now, everybody in the center of the living room, and, if anyone makes a move then the next time I shoot to kill."

Bear couldn't let things play out this way. If he did, they were all going to die.

He smelled the gasoline in the air and was halfway surprised the gunshot hadn't sparked a fire.

Right now, he needed to figure out what to do with Dell.

He glanced at his dad who still grasped his shoulder. Blood poured from the wound as his dad glowered at Dell.

"Hey, you." Dell pointed his gun at Bear. "I brought some rope with me." He reached into the pocket of his coat, pulled something out, and tossed it on the floor. "You need to start tying people up. Start with the men. One wrong move, and I think you know what's going to happen."

Bear stared at the rope and considered what he'd been asked to do.

Tying people up would take time. And time could buy him the opportunity to figure out a plan.

But once his family was bound . . . then there would be nothing they could do to help stop this man.

Bear raised his hands in the air as he stepped toward the rope. He tried his best to look inconspicuous. As he leaned down to grab the rope, a crash sounded in the distance.

Dell flung his head in that direction.

A lamp had hit the floor.

And that was just the distraction that Bear needed to make his move.

CHAPTER
FIFTY-TWO

PIPER WATCHED everything happen in slow motion.

The lamp fell from the table—after Piper had purposefully knocked it down.

Dell looked at her with narrowed eyes.

Raised his gun.

Finger on the trigger.

And the next instant, Bear tackled a distracted Dell.

Bear grabbed the man's wrist and slammed his hand into the floor.

The gun skidded across the room.

Isaac grabbed it.

Bear flipped Dell onto his stomach and jerked his arms behind him.

As he did that, Isaac grabbed the rope and began to tie Dell up.

Piper let out a breath, nearly sagging against the wall.

Was this really over?

Had the crisis really been diverted?

A sense of victory flooded her.

Maybe Dell would tell them where Julie was being kept.

Bear seemed to read her thoughts as he jerked Dell to his feet and shoved him against a wall. "Where's Julie?"

Dell smiled, blood trickling from the side of his mouth, as something close to amusement filled his gaze. "Wouldn't you like to know?"

"We need to call Shane," Isaac said. "We don't have any time to waste."

But just as Isaac reached into the basket of cells to grab his phone, something changed in the air.

And Piper knew that something was still wrong.

———

"Don't do that."

Bear looked up in time to see Luna standing in front of him.

She held a gun in her hand.

And it didn't belong to Dell.

She had come here with her own gun?

And now she was pointing it at . . . him?

"Put the gun down, or I'll shoot your brother," Luna told Isaac. "Don't test me."

Isaac stared at her a moment before slowly nodding and placing the gun on the floor.

"Now kick it toward me," Luna said. "I can't risk you getting any ideas."

Isaac used his foot to nudge the gun her way.

"Luna . . ." Piper muttered, her expression falling with disappointment.

Luna swung the gun toward her, her arms trembling. "Don't come closer. Don't make me do this."

"Why?" Piper asked. "Why are you helping this guy?"

Fire lit in her gaze. "You know I'm fascinated with serial killers. I talk about them all the time. One day, someone found me in an online forum I frequent. It's on the dark web. This person told me details about The Good Samaritan Killer—details I didn't know about. Eventually, we struck up a friendship."

"You're the one who's been helping Dell with the tech side of things," Piper muttered. "He recruited you."

Bear's mind raced. This couldn't be happening.

But it was.

"I wanted to be a part of the legacy." Luna's voice trembled. "I've never felt so much purpose as I did when I met Dell."

"And the reason he's always been two steps ahead of us is because you've been sharing what you know," Piper muttered, disgust filling her gaze. "You told him about Bear's meat allergy. Told him our schedule. Told him about what happened to me back in Chicago. It's been you all along."

Luna moved closer to Dell. "He's brilliant. I'm just sorry that no one else has been able to see it. But they will soon." Luna glanced at Bear. "Untie him."

Bear hesitated.

They'd just gotten this guy under control, and now they were supposed to release him?

"You heard the lady," Dell said. "Untie me."

Bear scowled as he reached behind the man.

This wasn't going to end this way. It couldn't.

Just as Bear reached for the rope, a loud pop sounded outside.

It almost sounded like an . . . explosion.

Realization filled him.

Something had set off that gasoline.

Bear knew that if he looked outside, he'd see a fire had started around his house.

CHAPTER
FIFTY-THREE

PIPER'S MIND RACED. She couldn't believe this was happening.

Luna?

Was she really involved with this?

Piper already knew the answer, but she could hardly believe it. She didn't want to believe it.

"You sought me out on purpose, didn't you?" Piper blurted.

"I did. I was actually keeping an eye on Bear, shadowing him so I could figure out what he knew and what was going on with his family." Her eyes sparkled. "It was a nice assignment. Eye candy, if you know what I mean. Anyway, I saw him meet with you, and I began doing some research. I figured out who you were. That's when I knew you'd be perfect for gleaning information."

"Luna . . ." Piper's voice cracked with emotion.

Luna's gaze darkened as she stared at Piper, a shadow seeming to cover her. "You didn't want to share information with me. You never asked for my opinion. Julie was your confidante, and you told me I had to put in my time first. I know way more than Julie ever did. I had so much to offer. Instead, all I got told was to get the coffee. File this. File that." She rolled her eyes. "It was so annoying."

"You were using me the whole time." Piper shook her head. She'd never thought of herself as someone who easily had the wool pulled over her eyes. But that's exactly what had happened.

Now, because of that, everyone in this room was in danger.

"I'm sorry." Luna shrugged, suddenly shifting back into nonchalant mode. "I really did enjoy learning under you. But this was an opportunity I couldn't pass up."

"Luna . . . you don't have to do this." Piper's voice trembled as she stared at the gun in her hands. "You have so much potential."

"I know. I don't *have* to do this. But I *want* to." She glanced back at Dell. "Is your camera still running?"

He glanced at his chest. "It should be."

"Perfect. We tweaked a few things, and we're recording this now." A sickly smile crossed Luna's lips. "Don't worry. I've been helping with edits. Dell did a decent job, but I'm helping him take it to the next level."

"You're not going to get away with this," Isaac said. "People are going to figure out what's going on."

"We know what we're doing." Dell's voice hardened.

"You're the one who poisoned Bear, aren't you, Luna?" Piper continued. "You must have put something on his food when you picked it up from the food truck."

Light gleamed in Luna's eyes. She was proud of what she'd done. She wanted the acknowledgement.

Maybe that would buy them some more time.

"I used powdered gelatin. I sprinkled a little on top, and it blended right in with the sauce. No one ever even knew. They just thought it was cross-contamination."

Of course. Gelatin was made from animal collagen. Eating any would have set off Bear's red meat allergy.

"How did you even know about alpha-gal?" Bear's chest heaved, making it clear adrenaline was pulsing through him and he was ready to act at a moment's notice.

"I do my research." Pride gleamed in Luna's eyes.

"You were quoted in an article about it several months ago, and I took notes. Knowledge is power, you know."

"And you're the one who leaked the story about Rebecca," Piper continued, more pieces clicking together. "How did you know?"

"When I came to Bear's place the first time, I left several listening devices so I could keep an ear on things." She scowled. "I left one in Bear's office and just happened to overhear a phone conversation between him and his brother about Rebecca. *How is she doing after what happened? I know she appreciates having you here.* Blah blah blah."

"Luna . . ." Piper muttered.

Her gaze flung back toward Piper's, fire in her eyes. "You would never tell me everything that was going on, so I had to resort to other measures. As soon as I heard what happened, I knew I had to exploit it. However, Dell deserves all the credit." She looked at him, her eyes beaming with admiration. "He's a brilliant man who's done brilliant things."

"He's not as smart as you think," Bear added as he met Dell's gaze. "You killed Lisa Moreno. Ralph cared about her. You two had a falling out, didn't you?"

Dell's gaze darkened. "Things were tense

between us for a while, but we both agreed that we could still work together on the mission."

"What mission is that?" James asked.

"To let people know they're not safe." Malice dripped from Dell's words. "I had other purposes. I found women who talked down to others. Who thought they were better than anyone else. Just like OJ thought he was better than me. Like my *mom* thought OJ was better than me. I had to show them they weren't anything special. In fact, those kinds of people make the world worse."

"You altered your MO," Piper said. "What changed?"

"Lots of things. Ralph was arrested, I met Luna, the doctor thought I had cancer. So many things put life into perspective." Dell shrugged as if it were all water under the bridge.

"Now, we need to stop talking!" Luna turned back to Bear and sneered. "What are you waiting for? I told you to untie Dell."

"These knots are tight." Bear gritted his teeth as he worked the rope. "You're going to have to give me a minute."

The next instant, Piper watched almost as if things happened in slow motion.

Bear shoved Dell toward Luna.

Luna panicked.

She pulled the trigger.

The bullet went into Dell, and he let out a gasp.

The gasp turned into a gurgle as he sank to his knees.

Isaac grabbed Luna's gun.

And as he did, Piper looked out the window just in time to see the flames flickering and spreading.

———

"Everyone, come on," Bear yelled. "We've got to get out of here. Now."

As he opened the door, he checked the progress of the fire around the perimeter of his house. They needed to hurry before their escape was blocked.

His dad was able to walk with Madison's help, even though he was still bleeding. Piper and Rebecca followed.

Once his family and loved ones were safe, he grabbed Dell and dragged the man outside as Isaac gripped Luna's arm.

Just as they reached the driveway, the blaze engulfed the house.

Bear watched everything he'd worked so hard for the past decade go up in flames.

But the important thing was that everybody was okay.

His gaze sought out Piper.

Piper stood with Rebecca, comforting her as tears flooded the woman's eyes.

Sirens sounded in the distance.

Had Shane figured things out?

It didn't matter.

All that mattered was that backup was on the way.

And maybe this would finally all be over.

FIFTY-FOUR

AS THE FBI and first responders filled the scene, Bear slipped an arm around Piper.

She nearly melted against him.

Luna was in the back of a police vehicle. His dad was being treated, and Dell was in an ambulance. Firefighters were busy putting out the flames.

"I'm so sorry, Piper," he murmured, his voice nearly hoarse as he leaned close enough that she could feel his breath on her ear. "I should have given you a chance to explain. It's just that—"

"I know." Her throat burned as she continued to lean into him. "It's hard to trust people after you've been burned."

"Will you forgive me?"

"Of course."

"I'm afraid that's something I'm going to have to

ask for more than just now. I'm going to make mistakes."

"We all do." She stepped back until she could see his face. Gently, she used her finger to trace the edge of his jaw. "That's what makes us all human, right?"

He stared at her a moment, his eyes swirling orbs of emotions. "It does."

She swallowed hard, feeling a lump in her throat. She could stare at Bear like this all day and be perfectly content.

"I'm just glad all of this is over," she said.

"Me too," Bear whispered.

His thick fingers tangled with her hair. The next instant, their lips met.

Piper hoped they'd have many more moments like this. Moments of bonding. Of celebrating. Of being together.

But without the danger.

Thank goodness, everyone had gotten out of the house safely.

But this wasn't over yet.

Another thought slammed into her mind.

"Where's Julie?" The words nearly croaked out of her mouth.

Bear sucked in a breath, and his gaze raced with thought. Finally, he turned back to her. "What if Dell was keeping her at his hunting cabin?"

"We need to go check. *Someone* needs to check." Urgency stained her voice.

"Let's find Shane."

———

As Agent Townsend hurried toward Dell's place, Bear and Piper sat in the back seat.

Townsend had agreed to let the two of them come as long as they stayed out of the way. While enroute, he explained that they'd talked to OJ Deerman, who'd mentioned that his brother, OD, had been obsessed with the GSK and had invested in a trail cam company.

When they'd looked further into the man, they'd discovered OD's timeline matched the killings. They'd gone to question him when they saw the smoke coming from Bear's place.

Thank goodness, they'd come when they did.

Once they arrived at Dell's cabin, Townsend and two other agents rushed toward it.

Piper and Bear climbed from the SUV and stood outside.

Bear squeezed Piper's hand as they waited, the minutes dragging by.

Was Julie inside? Piper prayed her friend was there. That she was okay.

A few minutes later, Townsend emerged with a woman beside him, a blanket wrapped over her shoulders.

The air left Piper's lungs.

Julie!

She rushed toward her friend and pulled her into a hug.

"Oh, Julie . . . are you okay?" Piper studied her friend's face, looking for any sign she was hurt.

Tears glistened in Julie's eyes. "I'm okay."

Piper hugged her again. "I'm so glad. And I'm so sorry this happened to you."

"It wasn't your fault," Julie said. "You couldn't have known."

"But—"

"No buts about it," Julie insisted. "Besides, I'm safe now. Thanks to you. The FBI agent said you never stopped looking for me. Thank you."

"I know you would have done the same thing for me."

Relief flooded Piper's heart.

Julie was okay. The Understudy had been arrested. Fog Lake was finally safe.

Maybe everyone could move on.

Finally.

EPILOGUE
THREE MONTHS LATER

BEAR SIGNED his name on the paperwork and stepped back from the conference table in their new office building.

Everyone in his family had added their signatures, and now it was official.

The Steadfast Justice Initiative had been formed.

As he put the pen down, Piper pulled a string on a party favor and streamers flew through the air. "I'm so excited for you guys." She grinned. "I truly am."

"And we're excited that you'll be helping us, Piper." James Colson stood in their circle, looking surprisingly content considering the hand life had given him.

The whole family had been moved into action. They wanted to do something for other people in their situation, so they'd started a nonprofit to help those unjustly imprisoned for crimes they didn't commit.

Between James Colson's personal experience, Isaac's legal expertise, Bear's cyber forensic skills, and Madison's compassionate heart and business-sense, they would be a perfect team.

Together, they could work hard to make sure others didn't go through the same struggles they had faced.

Between the compensation James received for being falsely imprisoned and through a monetary donation they'd received through Brynlee Wilder—Boone Wilder's wife and a local business owner—they'd been able to set up an office in downtown Fog Lake. Each of them would continue working their full-time jobs, and they'd take on clients on a case-by-case basis.

Rebecca picked up a cake from The Busy Bean and carried it toward the conference table. "We should celebrate."

They certainly had a lot to be grateful for.

Dell and Luna were now in jail.

Julie was safe.

Families who'd been mixed up in these crimes could finally begin to heal.

Bear stepped back and looked at the people in the room.

Andi and Makayla were here. They were Rebecca's cousins she was helping to raise. Now that Rebecca's dad had gone to get some help for his alcoholism, their home life was much more stable.

The fire had destroyed Bear's home. But at least everyone was safe. That was the important thing. Bear was staying at his childhood home while his house was being rebuilt, even bigger and better than before.

Tim had been fired from his position after it was revealed he'd altered that photo and placed money into an account set up in Piper's name. Even though Piper had been offered her old job back, she'd turned it down. Instead, she'd moved to Fog Lake where she would be consulting with the FBI as well as other law enforcement agencies. Now that her name had been cleared, work had been pouring in.

Daniel Barr, the man who'd been set free because of that photo, was being retried after another witness had stepped forward.

Julie was doing fine. She wasn't coming back as Piper's assistant, but she was going back to school. She and Piper kept in touch with each other, and Julie seemed to be recovering well.

It looked like everyone might have a happy ending after all.

"Can I have your attention?" Shane tapped on the edge of his glass, and everyone turned toward him.

Madison moved beside him, and Shane glanced at her, his face practically glowing.

"Madison and I just wanted to let you know that . . ." Shane took Madison's left hand and raised it in the air. "I proposed to Madison last night, and she said yes!"

Squeals and congratulations flooded the room.

"Now that we don't have the GSK and the Understudy to distract us, I'm hoping we can give our attention to planning a wedding." Madison wiggled her fingers to show off her ring. "I would love all of your help."

"Of course!" Rebecca gave her a hug.

"I'd love to," Piper added, waiting her turn to hug them.

For the first time in a long time, Bear felt joy in the air.

Finally, the stain in their lives seemed to be fading. Each of the Colsons would still be dealing with what had happened for a long time. But maybe they could finally put the past behind them and begin to heal.

Piper came and stood beside Bear. As she did, he took her hand in his and squeezed it.

He was so glad she was in his life . . . and he hoped he could prove that every day.

He leaned down and planted a quick kiss on her lips before whispering, "I love you."

She grinned as she stared up at him. "I love you too."

~~~

Thanks so much for reading *Refuge of Redemption*. I hope you enjoyed the book. If you did, would you please consider leaving a review?

ALSO BY CHRISTY BARRITT:

FOG LAKE SUSPENSE

Edge of Peril

When evil descends like fog on a mountain community, no one feels safe. After hearing about a string of murders in a Smoky Mountain town, journalist Harper Jennings realizes a startling truth. She knows who may be responsible—the same person who tried to kill her three years ago. Now Harper must convince the cops to believe her before the killer strikes again. Sheriff Luke Wilder returned to his hometown, determined to keep the promise he made to his dying father. The sleepy tourist area with a tragic past hadn't seen a murder in decades—until now. Keeping the community safe seems impossible as darkness edges closer, threatening to consume everything in its path. As The Watcher grows desperate, Harper and Luke must work together in order to defeat him. But the peril around them escalates, making it clear the killer will stop at nothing to get what he wants.

Margin of Error

Some secrets have deadly consequences. Brynlee Parker thought her biggest challenge would be hiking to Dead Man's Bluff and fulfilling her dad's last wishes. She never thought she'd witness two men being viciously murdered while on a mountainous trail. Even worse, the deadly predator is now hunting her. Boone Wilder wants nothing to do with Dead Man's Bluff, not after his wife died there. But he can't seem to mind his own business when a mysterious out-of-towner burst into his camp store in a frenzied panic. Something—or someone—deadly is out there. The killer's hunger for blood seems to be growing at a brutal pace. Can Brynlee and Boone figure out who's behind these murders? Or will the hurts and secrets from their past not allow for even a margin of error?

Brink of Danger

Ansley Wilder has always lived life on the wild side, using thrills to numb the pain from her past and escape her mistakes. But a near-death experience two years ago changed everything. When another incident nearly claims her life, she turns her thrill-seeking ways into a fight for survival. Ryan Philips left Fog Lake to chase adventure far from home. Now he's returned as the new fire chief in town, but the slower paced life he seeks is nowhere to be found. Not only is a wildfire blazing out of control, but a malicious killer known as "The Woodsman" is enacting crimes that appear accidental. Plus, there seems to be a strange connection with these incidents and his best friend's little sister, Ansley Wilder. As a killer watches their every move and the forest fire threatens to destroy their scenic town, both Ryan and Ansley hover on the brink of danger. One wrong move could send them tumbling over the edge . . . permanently.

Line of Duty

Jaxon Wilder didn't plan on returning home to Fog Lake, Tennessee, following his tour of duty in Iraq. But after a gut-wrenching failure during his stint in the Army, he now faces a new challenge: his family. Abby Brennan always did her best to be the good girl and to live by the rules. When a wrong decision changes her entire life, she tries to hide from the world. However, a madman known as the Executioner is determined to find her and enact his own brand of justice. When Jaxon and Abby are thrown together in the killer's crosshairs, they're forced to depend on one another to survive. Will Jaxon's sense of duty be enough to help keep Abby safe? Or will deadly secrets lead to the penalty of death?

Legacy of Lies

Madison Colson knows deep down that her father—a convicted serial killer—is innocent. But believing it and proving it are two entirely different things. Unable to help her father, Madison has spent most of her adult life overcompensating by helping others. When her aunt dies unexpectedly, duty calls her back to Fog Lake, Tennessee, a beautiful but painful place she'd rather forget. Terrifying events begin to unfold once she arrives, unleashing her worst nightmares. The Good Samaritan Killer—or a copycat—is back, and now Madison Colson is his target. FBI Special Agent Shane Townsend is determined to stop the deadly rampage that has sent the tight-knit community into a frenzy. But he needs to earn Madison's trust first. The task feels impossible, especially considering his father is the one who put her dad in prison. With the whole town on edge and pointing fingers, tension escalates out of control. Madison and Shane must sort the facts from the lies —and fight for a legacy of truth—before The Good Samaritan Killer has the final say.

Secrets of Shame

Attorney Isaac Colson only wants to put his tumultuous past in Fog Lake behind him and return to his life in Memphis. But when an ominous text threatens that he must come back or there will be deadly consequences, he knows he can't take any chances. Rebecca Moreno has only ever loved one man—her high school sweetheart, Isaac Colson. But when his dad went to prison for murder, Rebecca's father forbade them from seeing each other again. Years later, Isaac is back in town and old feelings are stirring. But Rebecca is harboring a secret that could change everything. When The Good Samaritan Killer strikes again, guilt pummels her. She has to tell Isaac the truth. But as events unfold, she has more to lose than ever. Isaac and Rebecca must find answers—their lives depend on it. But everyone seems to have secrets, each that forms an obstacle to finding the truth . . . and to staying alive.

YOU ALSO MIGHT ENJOY:

LANTERN BEACH MYSTERIES

Hidden Currents

You can take the detective out of the investigation, but you can't take the investigator out of the detective. A notorious gang puts a bounty on Detective Cady Matthews's head after she takes down their leader, leaving her no choice but to hide until she can testify at trial. But her temporary home across the country on a remote North Carolina island isn't as peaceful as she initially thinks. Living under the new identity of Cassidy Livingston, she struggles to keep her investigative skills tucked away, especially after a body washes ashore. When local police bungle the murder investigation, she can't resist stepping in. But Cassidy is supposed to be keeping a low profile. One wrong move could lead to both her discovery and her demise. Can she bring justice to the island . . . or will the hidden currents surrounding her pull her under for good?

Flood Watch

The tide is high, and so is the danger on Lantern Beach. Still in hiding after infiltrating a dangerous gang, Cassidy Livingston just has to make it a few more months before she can testify at trial and resume her old life. But trouble keeps finding her, and Cassidy is pulled into a local investigation after a man mysteriously disappears from the island she now calls home. A recurring nightmare from her time undercover only muddies things, as does a visit from the parents of her handsome ex-Navy SEAL neighbor. When a friend's life is threatened, Cassidy must make choices that put her on the verge of blowing her cover. With a flood watch on her emotions and her life in a tangle, will Cassidy find the truth? Or will her past finally drown her?

Storm Surge

A storm is brewing hundreds of miles away, but its effects are devastating even from afar. Laid-back, loose, and light: that's Cassidy Livingston's new motto. But when a makeshift boat with a bloody cloth inside washes ashore near her oceanfront home, her detective instincts shift into gear . . . again. Seeking clues isn't the only thing on her mind—romance is heating up with next-door neighbor and former Navy SEAL Ty Chambers as well. Her heart wants the love and stability she's longed for her entire life. But her hidden identity only leads to a tidal wave of turbulence. As more answers emerge about the boat, the danger around her rises, creating a treacherous swell that threatens to reveal her past. Can Cassidy mind her own business, or will the storm surge of violence and corruption that has washed ashore on Lantern Beach leave her life in wreckage?

Dangerous Waters

Danger lurks on the horizon, leaving only two choices: find shelter or flee. Cassidy Livingston's new identity has begun to feel as comfortable as her favorite sweater. She's been tucked away on Lantern Beach for weeks, waiting to testify against a deadly gang, and is settling in to a new life she wants to last forever. When she thinks she spots someone malevolent from her past, panic swells inside her. If an enemy has found her, Cassidy won't be the only one who's a target. Everyone she's come to love will also be at risk. Dangerous waters threaten to pull her into an overpowering chasm she may never escape. Can

Cassidy survive what lies ahead? Or has the tide fatally turned against her?

Perilous Riptide

Just when the current seems safer, an unseen danger emerges and threatens to destroy everything. When Cassidy Livingston finds a journal hidden deep in the recesses of her ice cream truck, her curiosity kicks into high gear. Islanders suspect that Elsa, the journal's owner, didn't die accidentally. Her final entry indicates their suspicions might be correct and that what Elsa observed on her final night may have led to her demise. Against the advice of Ty Chambers, her former Navy SEAL boyfriend, Cassidy taps into her detective skills and hunts for answers. But her search only leads to a skeletal body and trouble for both of them. As helplessness threatens to drown her, Cassidy is desperate to turn back time. Can Cassidy find what she needs to navigate the perilous situation? Or will the riptide surrounding her threaten everyone and everything Cassidy loves?

Deadly Undertow

The current's fatal pull is powerful, but so is one detective's will to live. When someone from Cassidy Livingston's past shows up on Lantern Beach and warns her of impending peril, opposing currents collide, threatening to drag her under. Running would be easy. But leaving would break her heart. Cassidy must decipher between the truth and lies, between reality and deception. Even more importantly, she must decide whom to trust and whom to fear. Her life depends on it. As danger rises and answers surface, everything Cassidy thought she knew is tested. In order to survive, Cassidy must take drastic measures and end the battle against the ruthless gang DH-7 once and for all. But if her final mission fails, the consequences will be as deadly as the raging undertow.

LANTERN BEACH ROMANTIC SUSPENSE

Tides of Deception

Change has come to Lantern Beach: a new police chief, a new season, and . . . a new romance? Austin Brooks has loved Skye Lavinia from the moment they met, but the walls she keeps around her seem impenetrable. Skye knows Austin is the best thing to ever happen to her. Yet she also knows that if he learns the truth about her past, he'd be a fool not to run. A chance encounter brings secrets bubbling to the surface, and danger soon follows. Are the life-threatening events plaguing them really accidents . . . or is someone trying to send a deadly message? With the tides on Lantern Beach come deception and lies. One question remains—who will be swept away as the water shifts? And will it bring the end for Austin and Skye, or merely the beginning?

Shadow of Intrigue

For her entire life, Lisa Garth has felt like a supporting character in the drama of life. The designation never bothered her—until now. Lantern Beach, where she's settled and runs a popular restaurant, has boarded up for the season. The slower pace leaves her with too much time alone. Braden Dillinger came to Lantern Beach to try to heal. The former Special Forces officer returned from battle with invisible scars and diminished hope. But his recovery is hampered by the fact that an unknown enemy is trying to kill him. From the moment Lisa and Braden meet, danger ignites around them, and both are drawn into a web of intrigue that turns their lives upside down. As shadows creep in, will Lisa and Braden be able to shine a light on the peril around them? Or will the encroaching darkness turn their worst nightmares into reality?

Storm of Doubt

A pastor who's lost faith in God. A romance

writer who's lost faith in love. A faceless man with a deadly obsession. Nothing has felt right in Pastor Jack Wilson's world since his wife died two years ago. He hoped coming to Lantern Beach might help soothe the ragged edges of his soul. Instead, he feels more alone than ever. Novelist Juliette Grace came to the island to hide away. Though her professional life has never been better, her personal life has imploded. Her husband left her and a stalker's threats have grown more and more dangerous. When Jack saves Juliette from an attack, he sees the terror in her gaze and knows he must protect her. But when danger strikes again, will Jack be able to keep her safe? Or will the approaching storm prove too strong to withstand?

Winds of Danger

Wes O'Neill is perfectly content to hang with his friends and enjoy island life on Lantern Beach. Something begins to change inside him when Paige Henderson sweeps into his life. But the beautiful newcomer is hiding painful secrets beneath her cheerful facade. Police dispatcher Paige Henderson came to Lantern Beach riddled with guilt and uncertainties after the fallout of a bad relationship. When she meets Wes, she begins to open up to the possibility of love again. But there's something Wes isn't telling her—something that could change everything. As the winds shift, doubts seep into Paige's mind. Can Paige and Wes trust each other, even as the currents work against them? Or is trouble from the past too much to overcome?

Rains of Remorse

A stranger invades her home, leaving Rebecca Jarvis terrified. Above all, she must protect the baby growing inside her. Since her estranged husband died suspiciously six months earlier, Rebecca has been determined to depend on no one but herself. Her chivalrous new neighbor appears to be an answer to prayer. But who is Levi Stoneman really? Rebecca wants to believe he can help her, but she can't ignore her instincts. As danger closes in, both Rebecca and Levi must figure out whom they can trust. With Rebecca's baby coming soon, there's no time to waste. Can the truth prevail . . . or will remorse overpower the best of intentions?

Torrents of Fear

The woman lingering in the crowd can't be Allison . . . can she? Because Allison was pronounced dead six years ago. Musician Carter Denver knows only one person who's capable of helping him find answers: Sadie Thompson, his estranged best friend and someone who also knew Allison. He needs to know if he's losing his mind or if Allison could have survived her car accident. Could Allison really be alive? If so, why is she trying to harm Carter and Sadie? As the two try to find answers, can Sadie keep her feelings for Carter hidden? Could he ever care for her, or is the man of her dreams still in love with the woman now causing his nightmares?

LANTERN BEACH PD

On the Lookout

When Cassidy Chambers accepted the job as police chief on Lantern Beach, she knew the island had its secrets. But a suspicious death with potentially far-reaching implications will test all her skills —and threaten to reveal her true identity. Cassidy enlists the help of her husband, former Navy SEAL Ty Chambers. As they dig for answers, both uncover parts of their pasts that are best left buried. Not everything is as it seems, and they must figure out if their John Doe is connected to the secretive group that has moved onto the island. As facts materialize, danger on the island grows. Can Cassidy and Ty discover the truth about the shadowy crimes in their cozy community? Or has darkness permanently invaded their beloved Lantern Beach?

Attempt to Locate

A fun girls' night out turns into a nightmare when armed robbers barge into the store where Cassidy and her friends are shopping. As the situation escalates and the men escape, a massive manhunt launches on Lantern Beach to apprehend the dangerous trio. In the midst of the chaos, a potential foe asks for Cassidy's help. He needs to find his sister who fled from the secretive Gilead's Cove community on the island. But the more Cassidy learns about the seemingly untouchable group, the more her unease grows. The pressure to solve both cases continues to mount. But as the gravity of the situation rises, so does the danger. Cassidy is determined to protect the island and break up the cult . . . but doing so might cost her everything.

First Degree Murder

Police Chief Cassidy Chambers longs for a break from the recent crimes plaguing Lantern Beach. She simply wants to enjoy her friends' upcoming wedding, to prepare for the busy tourist season about to slam the island, and to gather all the dirt she can on the suspicious community that's invaded the town. But trouble explodes on the island, sending residents—including Cassidy—into a squall of uneasiness. Cassidy may have more than one enemy plotting her demise, and the collateral damage seems unthinkable. As the temperature rises, so does the pressure to find answers. Someone is determined that Lantern Beach would be better off without their new police chief. And for Cassidy, one wrong move could mean certain death.

Dead on Arrival

With a highly charged local election consuming the community, Police Chief Cassidy Chambers braces herself for a challenging day of breaking up petty conflicts and tamping down high emotions. But when widespread food poisoning spreads among potential voters across the island, Cassidy smells something rotten in the air. As Cassidy examines every possibility to uncover what's going on, local enigma Anthony Gilead again comes on her radar. The man is running for mayor and his cult-like following is growing at an alarming rate. Cassidy feels certain he has a spy embedded in her inner circle. The problem is that her pool of suspects gets deeper every day. Can Cassidy get to the bottom of what's eating away at her peaceful island home? Will voters turn out despite the outbreak of illness plaguing their tranquil town? And the even bigger question: Has darkness come to stay on Lantern Beach?

Plan of Action

A missing Navy SEAL. Danger at the boiling point. The ultimate showdown. When Police Chief Cassidy Chambers' husband, Ty, disappears, her world is turned upside down. His truck is discovered with blood inside, crashed in a ditch on Lantern Beach, but he's nowhere to be found. As they launch a manhunt to find him, Cassidy discovers that someone on the island has a deadly obsession with Ty. Meanwhile, Gilead's Cove seems to be imploding. As danger heightens, federal law enforcement officials are called in. The cult's growing threat could lead to the pinnacle standoff of good versus evil. A clear plan of action is needed or the results will be devastating. Will Cassidy find Ty in time, or will she face a gut-wrenching loss? Will Anthony Gilead finally be unmasked for who he really is and be brought to justice? Hundreds of innocent lives are at stake . . . and not everyone will come out alive.

LANTERN BEACH BLACKOUT

Dark Water

Colton Locke can't forget the black op that went terribly wrong. Desperate for a new start, he moves to Lantern Beach, North Carolina, and forms Blackout, a private security firm. Despite his hero status, he can't erase the mistakes he's made. For the past year, Elise Oliver hasn't been able to shake the feeling that there's more to her husband's death than she was told. When she finds a hidden box of his personal possessions, more questions—and suspicions—arise. The only person she trusts to help her is her husband's best friend, Colton Locke. Someone wants Elise dead. Is it because she knows too much? Or is it to keep her from finding the truth? The Blackout team must uncover dark secrets hiding beneath seemingly still waters. But those very secrets might just tear the team apart.

Safe Harbor

Guilt over past mistakes haunts former Navy SEAL Dez Rodriguez. When he's asked to guard a pop star during a music festival on Lantern Beach, he's all set for what he hopes is a breezy assignment. Bree hasn't found fame to be nearly as fulfilling as she dreamed. Instead, she's more like a carefully crafted character living out a pre-scripted story. When a stalker's threats become deadly, her life—and career—are turned upside down. From the start, Bree sees her temporary bodyguard as a player, and Dez sees Bree as a spoiled rich girl. But when they're thrown together in a fight for survival, both must learn to trust. Can Dez protect Bree—and his carefully guarded heart? Or will their safe harbor ultimately become their death trap?

Ripple Effect

Griff McIntyre never expected his ex-wife and three-year-old daughter to come to Lantern Beach. After an abduction attempt, they're desperate for safety. Now Griff's not letting either of them out of his sight. Bethany knows Griff is the only one who can protect them, despite the fact that he broke her heart. But she'll do anything to keep her daughter safe—even if it means playing nicely with a man she can't stand. As peril ripples through their lives, Griff and Bethany must work together to protect their daughter. But an unseen enemy wants something from them . . . and will stop at nothing to get it. When disaster strikes, can Griff keep his family safe? Or will past mistakes bring the ultimate failure?

Rising Tide

Benjamin James knows there's a traitor within his former command. The rest of his team might even think it's him. As danger closes in, he must clear himself and stop a deadly plot by a dangerous terrorist group. All CJ Compton wanted was a new start after her career ended under suspicion. Working as the house manager for private security group

Blackout seems perfect. But there's more trouble here than what she left behind. As the tide rushes in, the stakes continue to rise. If the Blackout team fails, it's not just Lantern Beach at stake—it's the whole country. Can Benjamin and CJ overcome their differences and work together to find the truth?

LANTERN BEACH BLACKOUT: THE NEW RECRUITS

Rocco

Former Navy SEAL and new Blackout recruit Rocco Foster is on a simple in and out mission. But the operation turns complicated when an unsuspecting woman wanders into the line of fire. Peyton Ellison's life mission is to sprinkle happiness on those around her. When a cupcake delivery turns into a fight for survival, she must trust her rescuer—a handsome stranger—to keep her safe. Rocco is determined to figure out why someone is targeting Peyton. First, he must keep the intriguing woman safe and earn her trust. But threats continue to pummel them as incriminating evidence emerges and pits them against each other. With time running out, the two must set aside both their growing attraction and their doubts about each other in order to work together. But the perilous facts they discover leave them wondering what exactly the truth is . . . and if the truth can be trusted.

Axel

Women are missing. Private security firm Blackout must find them before another victim disappears. Axel Hendrix likes to live on the edge. That's why being a Navy SEAL suited him so well. But after his last mission, he cut his losses and joined Blackout instead. His team's latest case involves an undercover investigation on Lantern Beach. Olivia Rollins came to the island to escape her problems—and danger. When trouble from her past shows up in town, she impulsively blurts she's engaged to Axel, the womanizing man she's seen while waitressing. Now, she may not be the only one in danger. So could Axel. Axel knows Olivia might be his chance to find answers and that acting like her fiancé is the perfect cover for his latest assignment. But he doesn't like throwing Olivia into the middle of such a dangerous situation. Nor is he comfortable with the feelings she stirs inside him. With Olivia's life—as well as both their hearts—on the line, Axel must uncover the truth and stop an evil plan before more lives are destroyed.

Beckett

When the daughter of a federal judge is abducted, private security firm Blackout must find her. Psychologist Samantha Reynolds doesn't know why someone is targeting her. Even after a risky mission to save her, danger still lingers. She's determined to use her insights into the human mind to help decode the deadly clues being left in the wake of her rescue. Former Navy SEAL Beckett Jones needs to figure out who's responsible for the crimes hounding Sami. He's not sure why he's so protective of the woman he rescued, but he'll do anything to keep her safe—even if it means risking his heart. As the body count rises, there's no room for error. Beckett and Sami must both tear down the careful walls they've built around themselves in order to survive. If they don't figure out who's responsible, the madman will continue his death spree . . . and one of them might be next.

Gabe

When former Navy SEAL and current Blackout operative Gabe Michaels is almost killed in a hit-and-run, the aftermath completely upends his life. He's no longer safe—and he's not the only one. Dr. Autumn Spenser came to Lantern Beach to start fresh. But while treating Gabe after his accident, she senses there's more to what happened to him than meets the eye. When she digs deeper into his past, she never expects to be drawn into a deadly dilemma. Gabe has been infatuated with the pretty doctor since the day they met. Now, can he keep her from harm? Could someone out of his league ever return his feelings or will her past hurts keep them apart? As danger continues to pummel them, Gabe and Autumn are thrown together in a quest to find answers. More important than their growing attraction, they must stay alive long enough to stop the person desperate to destroy them.

ABOUT THE AUTHOR

USA Today has called Christy Barritt's books "scary, funny, passionate, and quirky."

Christy writes both mystery and romantic suspense novels that are clean with underlying messages of faith. Her books have won the Daphne du Maurier Award for Excellence in Suspense and Mystery, have been twice nominated for the Romantic Times Reviewers' Choice Award, and have finaled for both a Carol Award and Foreword Magazine's Book of the Year.

She is married to her Prince Charming, a man who thinks she's hilarious—but only when she's not trying to be. Christy is a self-proclaimed klutz, an avid music lover who's known for spontaneously bursting into song, and a road trip aficionado.

When she's not working or spending time with her family, she enjoys singing, playing the guitar, and exploring small, unsuspecting towns where people have no idea how accident-prone she is.

Find Christy online at:
   www.christybarritt.com
   www.facebook.com/christybarritt
   www.twitter.com/cbarritt

Sign up for Christy's newsletter to get information on all of her latest releases here: **www.christybarritt. com/newsletter-sign-up/**

Made in United States
Orlando, FL
13 September 2024